CONFLICT OF EMOTIONS

Geraldine McCall

CONFLICT OF EMOTIONS
Copyright © 2023 Geraldine McCall.

Authorunit
17130 Van Buren Blvd., Ste. 238,
Riverside, CA 92504
877-826-5888
www.authorunit.com

ISBN 978-1-960075-20-8 (Paperback)
ISBN 978-1-960075-21-5 (Ebook)

Printed in the United States of America

Contents

About
Conflict of Emotions

*T*his is the story of a woman who pays too high a price for love. At first glance, Janice and Christopher Blunt seem to have the ideal marriage; in fact, Janice's love for Chris is so strong that she foregoes the pursuit of a higher education to marry him. They have three beautiful children, a home, and a great deal of happiness–or so it seems.

As the years pass, Janice notices a change in Chris, but tries to smooth over any disagreements in the hopes that their love will remain strong. Because Janice's belief in the sanctity of marriage and the commitment it entails is so strong, she refuses to face reality and see Chris for what he really is: a liar and an adulterer who has repeatedly taken advantage of his wife's trusting nature.

The true conflict of emotions comes when Janice has no choice but to face the truth about her husband. The enormity of the decision she must make–a decision affecting every facet of her life–threatens to render her helpless, causing her great mental and physical anguish. Janice's choice–and the grace and dignity with which she carries it out–will serve as an inspiration to all those forced to choose between their belief in the sacred union of marriage and their own personal happiness.

Chapter One

Janice was headstrong as a child and more so as a teenager. After church on Sunday nights she was supposed to go straight home. Not once did she go directly home.

Janice almost always rode with her best friend, Minnie Laws, after church. Every Sunday night, Minnie asked Janice if she was going home. Janice would answer, "No, I am going to the Palace." Janice's parents did not own a car, so she walked to church and a church member would give her a ride home. Usually, Minnie took her wherever she wanted to go.

As Minnie and Janice pulled up to the Palace one evening, Minnie said, "I am lucky tonight, there is a parking space right in front."

The Palace was a gathering place for teenagers. It consisted of a small restaurant with a large room at the side; this room had a jukebox and plenty of dancing space. The dancing area opened on three sides, and each side had roll-up doors that looked like those found on garages. As a matter of fact, the whole place had a used-to-be-a-garage look about it.

The music played loud enough to be heard several blocks away. Janice did not know how to dance, but she enjoyed watching the dancers and being with her friends.

Janice and Minnie had been at the Palace for twenty minutes when a young man asked Minnie to dance. Minnie smiled and walked to the dance floor. Another young man asked Janice to dance. She did not want to tell him she did not know how to dance. Without delay, she said, "I do not dance with young men I don't know."

"My name is Christopher Blunt." Janice looked around and started walking off. Chris grabbed her arm, "You are not being fair. I've told you my name, why not tell me yours?"

Janice said, "We have not been properly introduced." "I told you my name," he replied.

"Yes, you gave me a name, but you will have to be introduced to me by someone I know and someone who knows you. Now, will you please leave me alone?"

Chris walked away. Janice thought she had seen the last of him. A few minutes later, he came back – but not alone.

"Do you know her?" Chris asked the young man with him.

"Sure, I know her," the young man said smiling in Janice's direction. Chris looked at Janice and asked, "Do you know Harold?" She looked at Harold and said, "Everyone knows Harold Thomas."

Harold said, "Janice, I would like you to meet a nice young man." He placed his hand on Chris's shoulder and pushed him closer to her. "This is Chris Blunt. Chris, this is Janice Scruggs."

Janice placed her hand in Chris's hand, smiled and said, "It's nice to meet you, Chris."

Again Chris asked her to dance. She told him that she had never learned to dance.

"I'll be glad to teach you to dance," he said, pulling her toward the dance floor. "Just follow the steps I make; I will lead and you will follow. If you step on my foot, I won't notice." He placed his arm around her waist and said, "Listen to the music and follow my lead."

The song playing was "Your Precious Love," by Jerry Butler. Before the record had ended, Janice felt as thought she were floating on air. Chris was so easy to follow. She thought of the fun she had been missing because she had always been too shy to learn to dance. I will never be called a wallflower again, she thought.

Before the night was over, Janice knew she would like to see Chris again.

They made a date for the next weekend.

Janice's parents did not care for Chris. He had the reputation of being a Romeo. In addition, he had dropped out of Dillard High School during his senior year. They discussed their feelings, and left the final decision to her. As a result, she dated Chris every weekend. However, she was not permitted to date during the week. For their dates, Chris borrowed his older brother's station wagon – affectionately called "Woody" —drove to Pompano and picked her up, then he drove back to Fort Lauderdale. As they drove along, she could see the road through the large hole in the floor.

Sixth Street Sundry, on the corner of Northwest Sixth Street and Ninth Avenue was the most popular teenager hangout in Fort Lauderdale. If Chris and Janice did not go to the Thunderbird Drive-In, they danced and ate hamburgers at the Sundry.

After Janice graduated form Blanche Ely High School, she could not decide which college she wanted to attend. She and Minnie talked on the telephone for hours, discussing different colleges. They finally decided it would be either Florida A&M University (FAMU) in Tallahassee or Clark College in Atlanta, Georgia. They eventually chose FAMU.

After Janice and Minnie agreed on a college, Janice informed her parents of their choice. Everything became one big rush: hurry and get your physical, hurry and fill out the papers for the college. Still, Janice enjoyed all the planning she and Minnie had to do.

At last everything was settled: Janice and Minnie would be roommates.

They planned to leave for Tallahassee at the end of August.

In the meantime, Chris had been asking Janice if she really wanted to attend school away from home. "Why not go to Broward Junior College for two years, then switch to a four-year institution?" he asked.

In addition to the pressure from Chris, Janice's mother said to her, "If only you were not going to college, I could buy another house." Janice's family lived in a wooden house and her mother wanted to purchase a home made with concrete. She asked, "Mom, would you prefer another house? I can stay home and get a job. Maybe I could start college next year."

"No," answered Mrs. Scruggs. "I want you to get an education so you can better your position in life."

From time to time, Chris asked her to consider attending a local college.

Janice began to feel she was being pulled in two directions at once. Her mother wanted another home and Chris did not want her to go away to school.

One particular evening, Chris and Janice had been to the Thunderbird Drive-In. As they drove toward the Burger King on Sunrise Boulevard, Janice asked, "Chris, why do you want me to stay at home and attend our local college?"

"Because if you go away, I feel it may be the end of our relationship. I don't want to lose you. I love you and want you to be my wife."

"Are you asking me to marry you?" she whispered.

"Yes, I am," he answered, turning the car into Sunland Park instead of the Burger King parking lot. He drove past the swimming pool and the park building, eventually coming to a stop under the branches of a low-hanging tree. He turned to Janice and pulled her into his arms, "I am twenty-one years old. I have been trying to ask you to marry me for the last two weeks, but you have been so excited about going away to school that I didn't want to deprive you of what you seem to want most."

Janice began to laugh and cry at the same time. Finally she calmed down enough to say, "I took it for grated that we would wait until I competed my education before getting married. I need some time to get my thoughts in order."

"Take all the time you need, sweetheart, just give me an answer before the end of the week. I want to settle down and start a family."

The next day at lunch, Janice told Minnie, "I have a problem and need to discuss it with someone."

"What is it? Maybe I can help."

Janice hesitated, "Mom keeps saying she wants to buy another house. Whenever I tell her to go ahead and buy the house, she tells me that she wants me to go to college so I can better my position in life —and to make matters worse, Chris wants me to marry him. I am being pulled in two directions!"

"Deep down," Janice continued, "I don't feel I am ready to go away from home. I have never been away from home for more than one weekend at a time—and the first semester is three months long. If I go to school, I'll feel as if I am depriving my mother of the home she wants. I may take the easy way out and marry Chris."

"Marriage is a serious step," said Minnie. "Be sure it is what you really want; don't use it as an escape. If you really want to go to school, go. If you would rather get married, then by all means get married. Make up your own mind, but remember: the decision you make now will affect you for a lifetime."

Later in the day, as Janice and Chris talked on the telephone, she said, "I have decided to marry you instead of going to college."

"Do you want me to come up tonight and talk to your parents?" he asked.

"No, I will talk to them," Janice said. "My father will accept whatever decision I make. My mother is the one I am worried about."

"Good luck in talking to your mother. If you need me, I'll be by the telephone; call me when you have spoken with your parents."

When Janice told her parents of her decision to get married, her father accepted it without argument. Mrs. Scruggs fumed and argued. "I will not sign any papers consenting to your marriage. You are only eighteen and I will not sign for you to marry. In this state, you must be twenty-one to marry without your parents' consent—and I will not sign."

Turning to Janice, Mrs. Scruggs asked, "Why do you insist on throwing your life away? That man will never amount to anything, and neither will you without a proper education."

Two months later, Chris told Janice he had enlisted in the U.S. Army; he would be leaving for basic-training camp within the next two weeks. "I would like to be married before I leave. Try to convince your mother that she should not keep us from getting married," he implored.

After much pleading and crying, Mrs. Scruggs finally gave in and consented to the marriage. They were married at the Broward County Courthouse four days before Chris entered the Army.

Chris had been gone one month when Janice realized she was pregnant. During his tour in the army, Chris came home every two months, and sixteen month after Wendolyn's birth, Janice gave birth to Beverly.

At the end of two years, Chris received an honorable discharge from Uncle Sam. A month after Chris's discharge from the Army, Janice was pregnant again.

During the two years Chris had been in the Army, Janice had worked at a local laundry. Saving the monthly check she received from Uncle Sam, she and the girls had lived off her salary from the laundry.

Chris had been home a few weeks when his pocket money ran out. Janice gave him the bankbook to replenish his funds for bus transportation and lunches while he looked for employment. After five months, Chris was still looking for work. He could not find the type of job he wanted, he kept telling her.

One day as she was hanging up a jacket Chris had left lying on the bed, she heard something fall to the floor. Picking up the item, she saw the long- forgotten savings passbook. Opening the passbook, her heart began to pound as she noted the one-hundred dollar balance. Feeling faint, she collapsed onto the double bed. Where has all the money gone?

Getting up, Janice forced herself to remain in control. Keep calm in front of the children, she repeated over and over as she waited for Chris to come home. She kept her mind busy by playing a game of Old Maids with the children. The children did not notice that their mother was not paying full attention to the game.

Janice was in bed when Chris came home. Turning her soft brown eyes towards him she asked, "Chris, what happened to the money we had in the bank? I was hanging up your jacket and the passbook fell out. Looking in it, I noticed there was only one hundred dollars remaining in the account."

"I needed the money for bus fare and lunches while job hunting. I am usually on the beach when lunch time comes, and it is expensive out there."

"You should try taking a lunch with you. I don't understand how lunch and bus fare could cost over two thousand dollars."

After getting no answer, Janice continued. "Chris, since most of the money is gone, why don't we take the remaining hundred dollars and use it as a down payment on a car? We will always need transportation."

Chris was not sure what he thought of this idea, but he readily agreed in order to avoid starting a heated fight.

"You know that's not a bad idea."

Within a month, they were the proud owners of their first vehicle, and Chris had his first full-time job since being discharged. His new job was working at a service station on the corner of Seventh Avenue and Sixth Street, pumping gas, on the three-to-eleven shift.

When Chris began working he was happy giving Janice his paycheck every Friday. She cashed his check, paid the bills and divided the remainder between them.

He spent his money during the weekend. He visited local bars and night clubs. She stayed home with the children. Janice did not drink alcohol. She spent her money on chewing gum and used books.

Every Monday morning Chris asked, "Baby, how much money do you have?" when she replied he asked for half of whatever her answer was.

Week in and week out Chris came to her every Monday morning for half of her spending money. He was caught off-guard on this particular day when she replied, "No I don't have any money to give you."

"What! What do you mean you don't have any money? What did you do with it?"

"I didn't do anything with it and I am not giving it to you. Every weekend you spend your money and take half of mine. You need to learn to live with your half and not count on spending mine."

"I need gas there is no gas in the car."

"Call your co-worker John before he leaves for work," she instructed.

Chris began spending weekends at home; he stopped visiting clubs and bars.

One friday night after returning from work, Chris woke Janice to tell her what had happened that night at the station. It seemed that two men pulled up to the pump and asked for five dollars' worth of high-test. As Chris stood at the rear of the vehicle pumping gas, he looked through the rear window and saw a couple kissing. Looking at the hose to make sure the nozzle was in the neck of the gas tank, he again glanced through the rear window. Seeing that the couple was still joined in an embrace, he looked closer and realized he was looking at two men embracing.

Dropping the hose, Chris started to run toward the office of the service station. As the two men heard the gas pump strike the pavement, they loosened their hold on each other and glanced around. Starting to laugh, the driver pulled a bill from his wallet and pushed it through the window, saying, "Here is the money for the gas."

"Keep it," Chris yelled at him. "I don't want it." Still laughing, the car pulled onto Seventh Avenue.

When Chris had finished his story, both he and Janice had a good laugh. "I don't mind having to pay the money for the gas—I was just scared of getting too close to those two."

Babe," interrupted Janice, "You have a letter on the dresser." "Who is it from?" he inquired.

"It's from Ave and Hughie King in New York."

Reaching for the letter and tearing it open, he paused after reading part of the letter and said, "Honey, they want to come to Florida for their vacation this summer."

"Great," replied Janice. "I have never met them and they have never been to Florida. We should all enjoy ourselves."

Chris finished reading the letter, and then placed a call to New York.

Chapter Two

Fort Laurendale, with its beautiful Atlantic beaches, fantastic climate year- round, and unlimited entertainment and recreational facilities, provides a setting that is unequal in the United States. Fort Lauderdale is located in Broward County, which is serviced by the Fort Lauderdale-Hollywood International Airport, open twenty-four hours a day. Charter services and flying schools are also available. It maintains an extensive interconnecting public-transit system, including a special "beach buggy" that travels A-1-A along the curving, palm-fringed ocean. Bus service starts in Pompano Beach, passes through Fort Lauderdale, and ends in Hallandale about eight miles to the south of Fort Lauderdale.

Driving away from Miami International Airport after picking up Ave and Hughie, Janice said to Chris. "Honey, when we get to Fort Lauderdale, Don't turn west until we get to Las Olas Boulevard. I want them to see those houses on the islands. That place will blow their minds."

Sure enough, as they drove west on Las Olas Boulevard, Hughie exclaimed, "Blunt, slow down! How do these trees get like that?"

"What do you mean Hughie?" Chris inquired.

"I mean, how does that green stuff get to the top of the palm trees? Does someone climb up there and wrap the green stuff around the top of the trees?"

Not yet understanding what Hughie was trying to say, Chris looked up at the trees along the Boulevard and started to laugh. "Hughie," Chris said, "the royal palms grow that way. Look at the smaller tree; it's called a coconut palm. Do you see those things at the top of the tree, just below the long palm fronds?"

"Yes, I see them. What are they?"

"Those are coconuts before they are taken from the husk. You are used to seeing them already husked."

"Well, I'll be damned! Who would have guessed that they would look like that?"

As they continued driving, Ave exclaimed, "This is where I plan to move when I retire from the school system of New York. I am going to live out here on one of these islands. There is nothing in this world more beautiful than these homes and the shrubbery. Down here I can have plants that bloom all year round—and I would not have to cover them with burlap or anything else. Oh, to live without snow all year round—what a beautiful thought!"

As they continued westward along the Boulevard, Janice said, "This is an exclusive shopping area. There are boutiques on both sides of the street. Look at the well-manicured grass along the sidewalks. Over there is an unusual drug store; you will also find gourmet food shops and stores that import toys and games. Some stores specialize in wicker furnishings, custom-designed fabrics, paintings and sculptures, fine antiques, and the most gorgeous Florida fashions and European designs. Anything you want you should be able to find on Las Olas Boulevard. We also have commercial shopping centers, for people in my price range."

From the front passenger seat, Hughie glanced over his left shoulder, "I hear that whenever you want an orange here in Florida, all you have to do is stick your hand out the nearest window and pull one from the tree. Do you have orange trees in your yard?"

"No," she replied, "We live in an apartment complex, and there are no fruit trees there. We plan to make sure you have plenty of fruit during your visit, and we would like for you to take as much fruit as you can carry back with you. Is there anything special you would like to see and do during your visit? We made up a suggested itinerary, but please feel free to change it if we have left anything out."

Hughie replied, "I want to see the Everglades. I have always heard about the Everglades, and I don't intend to go back to New York without going out there. Ave, what would you like to see down here?"

'I would like to see everything. This is my first visit to the Sunshine State, so whatever I see will be new to me. I would like to shop—just turn me loose in a shopping center with the checkbook and I will be fine."

During the week, Ave and Hughie were invited to house parties held by friends of Chris and Janice. At one of the parties, Ave and Hughie played a game that none of the Floridians had heard of before called Black Magic, and everyone had a hilarious time. Along with the nighttime festivities, they visited almost every tourist attraction in Fort Lauderdale, Palm Beach, and Miami.

One afternoon, the two families toured Lion Country Safari. After getting their tickets at the main entrance, they drove a short distance to allow another attendant to tear the stub portion off their tickets. As Chris pulled up to give the attendant the admission tickets, Ave said, "Look, Blunt, there is a large ostrich standing next to the attendant."

Stopping in front of the man, Chris did not open the window. After a few minutes, the attendant tapped on the window and said, "Roll the window down; I have to tear the stub off your tickets."

"Will that thing bite?" Chris asked, pointing to the ostrich.

"No, he is trained to tear the stubs from your ticket. All you need to do is hold tightly to your end and the ostrich will tear the stub without touching you."

"He won't tear these tickets because I am not dumb enough to stick my hand in that bird's mouth."

"Give the ticket to me," said Janice. "I am not afraid of him." Chris handed the tickets across the seat, saying, "If you lose a couple of fingers, I won't say I told you so."

Reaching her hand through the back window, the big ostrich tore the tickets in half with one swift pull of its strong beak.

"Hughie, will you check and make sure my wife still has both hands? One may be missing," Chris said as he continued driving slowly through the African attraction. Soon they noticed a group of lions lying in the shade of a tree.

"Those are the laziest group of wild animals I have ever seen," said Hughie. "They look so peaceful."

"If you had to lie in that hot place all day, you wouldn't have any energy, either," replied Ava. "We are riding in an air-conditioned car."

Continuing around the safari grounds, they came to an area where patrons could pet and hand-feed the livestock. The adults allowed the children to feed and play with the animals; then they climbed into the car and returned to Fort Lauderdale.

By the end of the week, Janice and Chris were glad to wave goodbye to the jet carrying their friends back to the Big Apple.

Two weeks after Ave and Hughie returned to New York, Chris and Janice's third child was born. Janice gave Chris the honor of naming his first son—Rodney Bernard Blunt.

The next few years were a happy time for the entire family, and for Minnie who married Thomas Campfield.

Chapter Three

Janice was in the habit of keeping the front door to their apartment locked and continually reprimanded the children for leaving the door unlocked. One Halloween Chris heard her instructing the children to always lock the door after they came in from outside.

"There is no need to keep the door locked when I am home," he said. "I won't allow any harm to come to my family."

"It is still a safe practice to keep the doors around here locked," Janice replied.

Later that evening, Janice was sitting on the sofa reading, Chris was sitting next to her watching a baseball game. "I don't like leaving the door unlocked," she said as she glanced uneasily up from her book.

"I am home; don't worry," he replied. "This is Halloween and I am sick and tired of getting up every few minutes to open the door."

At this time, the front door slowly began to open. "Someone is opening the door," Janice said in a frightened voice.

"Don't worry," Chris said on his way to the door. "It's just some kids that forgot their manners about knocking, and did not say "Trick-or-Treat.'"

The door was opened much wider before Chris reached it, what he saw caused him to stop in his tracks. A person with an ugly mask with horribly distorted facial features was limping into the apartment. He had his right hand stretched before him, and the hand seemed to be covered with blood; he also had on a yellow terrycloth bathrobe, which was belted at the waist, and the belt was dragging on the floor as he walked; he was bent at the waist, and the back of this unknown person had a large hump on the right shoulder. Seeing this, Chris yelled, "What the hell?" and ran as fast as he could toward the back door.

Janice stood, realized that this was Halloween, laid her Agatha Christie novel facedown on the sofa, and glanced past the hunchbacked figure to see Minnie standing behind the ugly figure, bent over and laughing as hard as she could. Janice said to Chris, "Come back, brave man. It's only Minnie and Tom playing a joke on us."

During this time, the children had backed into the corner behind the television set, hugging each other and crying.

Tom could hold his laughter no longer. He pulled the ugly mask from his face, stood straight, and said to the children, "This is only catsup on my hands; don't be frightened. I wanted to teach your dad that it didn't matter if he was home or not, it is no longer safe to leave a door unlocked, no matter how short the time you will be away."

Returning to the room, laughing, Chris said, "I knew it was some fool; I just wasn't sure which fool it was. How the hell did you get the hump on your back?"

"This is a pillow Minnie strapped on with a belt; it was her idea to do this. She wanted to see which one of you would be the first to run if trouble started."

"Why aren't you out with the children 'Trick-or-Treating'?" Minnie asked Janice, as she watched the children settle in front of the television again.

"I took them to Pompano earlier in the evening; we stopped at different friends homes, and we stopped at every Seven-Eleven between Fort Lauderdale and Pompano. I don't allow them to go out alone, because of strangers, nor do I take them to the homes of people I don't know.

They have enough candy anyway," Janice replied, then asked, "Where are your children?"

"They went to a Halloween party at a neighbor's house. We dropped them off and will pick them up later."

"Some people need to keep a closer watch on their children. On our way here, right down the street from you, we saw a group of children throwing eggs on cars. I know their parents can't be aware of some of the things children get into when they are not around," Minnie said, then continued, "You are not the only family we plan to play this joke on, which means we cannot remain here very long." They visited for a short time, then left.

Chapter Four

One evening, Chris came home from work to a very agitated wife. "Honey, what is wrong? Are you all right?"

"I am upset because our rent has been raised again. Everything goes up except the almighty paycheck. I am sick to death of paying out our hard- earned money to a rent man who gets all the tax breaks."

Taking a quick breath, she continued, "I want a house. At least then we could claim the homestead exemption. I am sick and tired of making the man richer. They are building a new subdivision not far from here. Let's go out there and apply for one of those houses."

"Calm down, baby," Chris said. "I will find out what I can about owning our own home and get back to you. In the meantime, just calm down. We will have to pay the higher rent, there is nothing else we can do at the present time."

Chris did not want the responsibility of a house and hoped Janice would forget about owning a home. He immediately forgot about his promise. Consequently, a few weeks later he was surprised to hear her ask, "Did you get any information about the homes that we talked of a couple of weeks ago?"

"Yes, I found out that I don't want one. Everyone I have talked to who has his own place complained about how expensive the upkeep of a home is. Your work is never done when you own your own place. One guy even said that buying a home was the biggest mistake he ever made."

"Be that as it may," she replied, "you don't sleep with your male friend, you sleep with me. I am telling you here and now, I want a house and I want it as soon as our credit is approved. And I'll tell you this: if you don't get me a house, I'll find some woman's son who will. All you damn men ever want is a new car parked at an apartment building; you don't want a home because it means less time to spend running the streets. Don't you realize we will never stop paying rent? The only way out is to acquire property for ourselves."

"Woman, I am tired of your mouth. We won't be able to pay off a house either. We will be dead before we're able to pay off a mortgage," he yelled.

"That is the stupidest thing I ever heard. If we die before the mortgage is paid in full, the insurance will pay it off and our children will own it. How the hell do you think the man got over? Look at all those old houses on the beach—they have long been paid for. Now those people can live on easy street. They pay the taxes without having a mortgage to worry about in their old age. On top of that, you may be dumb enough to die, but I won't. I will be right there, enjoying my house."

"There is no reasoning with you," Chris yelled again. "You are as stubborn and headstrong as a raging bull. I won't buy a house. Now leave me alone!"

Needless to say, six months later they moved into their new home.

Chapter Five

After moving into their new home, Janice decided to give Chris the privilege of paying the household bills. She sat with him at the dining room table and instructed him on depositing money into their checking account, filling in the memo area and how to reconcile the bank statement.

"After learning how to do this, how do you feel about handling the money and paying bills?"

"It will be a breeze, it's simple, anyone can do it; on top of that, if I have questions all I have to do is ask you."

Almost every Sunday, Janice and Chris took their children for a drive. One Sunday they drove north, and the next Sunday they drove south, or east, or west. On this particular Sunday, they decided to drive south to Crandon Park Zoo in Miami. The children always enjoyed looking at the animals. Chris bought peanuts for the children to feed the monkeys.

"Look," cried Wendy, after they entered the zoo, "that ugly monkey looks like a rainbow." Looking where Wendy was pointing, they saw a large baboon hanging from an iron bar across the top of the shelter where he lived. The hair around his neck was white mixed with gray, his main body hair was brown, and the hair around his rear end was pink.

"He is funny looking," stated Beverly. "Daddy, what kind of monkey is that? Should I give him some peanuts?"

"Don't give him anything," replied Chris. "Throw some on the floor of the cage and see what he does; he may not be friendly."

Beverly threw a handful of nuts on the floor of the cage. Seeing her drop the peanuts, worked as a signal, prompting the monkey to go into action. He dropped to the floor, pouncing on the peanuts as if they were the most delicate of delicacies. His actions were so fast and funny that everyone in the small group around the cage began to laugh. The monkey looked up, made a face, and patted his rear end at the own-lookers.

"That is the end of his show kids. Let's move on to the alligator pit," Chris said and walked away.

The sun was scorching hot. "This sure doesn't feel like winter to me," said Chris. "We must be closer to the equator than the scientists think we are."

On their way home from Crandon Park Zoo, Chris said to Janice, "The children seem to love animals. Why don't we give some thought to getting them a pet?"

"That's a good idea," she replied. "What animal would you suggest?" "Any animal except a cat; I don't like cats. Have you ever noticed how a cat's eyes look in the dark? They seem to look right into your soul," he said, a frown upon his handsome face.

"I'll get a pet that won't need much care. I know that when the novelty wears off, I will be the one taking care of the pet," Janice said.

A few days later she arrived home with an aquarium and all the paraphernalia needed—plus both tropical fish and goldfish. Chris looked up from playing solitaire on the floor of the den, saw what she had brought and demanded, "Janice, why the devil did you get tropical fish and goldfish, they cannot get along with one another—the tropical fish will kill the goldfish."

"I don't think so; the man in the Fish Bowl said they could live together."

"He would probably tell you anything to make a sale."

Hearing this, the children came running, yelling, "Goldfish! Goldfish! Momma brought us goldfish!"

"All right children, I need your help in setting up the tank. Who volunteers to help me?"

"I do, I do," they said in unison.

"Let's start. Wendy, you can put the water in the tank; Beverly, after Wendy has the water in the tank, put two drops of the chlorine in the tank to take the fluoride out of the water. In the meantime, you and Rodney fix up the charcoal and filter. I'll get the rocks and plants ready to place in the bottom of the tank."

Instantly, everyone was busy. Wendy placed the fish tank on the counter in the kitchen and started filling a pot with water. Chris was playing solitaire in the den, looking up ever so often, as if he was supervising everything. Beverly, Rodney and Janice arranged charcoal, filter, rocks and plants in containers and groups. Everyone was pleased with the final results.

As the weather began to turn cold, Janice decided to get a heater for the fish tank. She stopped by the Fish Bowl, told the proprietor what she wanted, and he showed her the different heaters. Janice purchased one of medium price. A few days later, she saw Chris at the fish tank with the heater in his hand.

"What are you doing?" she asked.

"I'm seeing how the thermostat works on the heater." He continued toying with the heater a few minutes longer; then walked away.

"Did you leave the heater the way you found it?" she inquired.

"Yes, I did. Stop worrying about the fish being cold," he said over his shoulder.

Later in the evening, she asked Chris if he wanted to go to Pompano to visit her parents. The children overheard as usual, and yelled, "Yes, we want to visit Nana and Granddaddy."

Chris picked up his jacket and said, "All right, let's go."

Shortly after arriving, Janice and her mother had gone into the bedroom to catch up on the latest family gossip. Concerned about her daughter, Mrs. Scruggs asked, "Janice, how have you been feeling lately?"

"Not too spiffy Mom. I am going to make an appointment to see the doctor. Let's go back into the den where the men are."

As they entered the den, a loud, piercing scream came through the window. Everyone rushed to the back yard. Wendy and Rodney were under the mango tree, looking up and pointing. Janice looked and saw Beverly hanging from two branches. The fingers of both hands were wrapped around one branch, her toes barely touching a lower limb. As Janice looked closer she saw the skirt of Beverly's dress was caught by a shorter limb; she could not move further because the branch held her dress too tightly. Beverly knew if she turned the upper branch loose, she would fall to the ground.

Chris too saw the dilemma Beverly was in and grabbed a ladder from the side of the house. He leaned the ladder on the trunk of the tree and climbed towards his terrified daughter. As he reached her, she let out another terrified scream and jumped into Chris's arms, wherefore the ladder started to shake, scaring Beverly even more. Chris grabbed onto a branch of the mango tree with one hand, steadying himself and the ladder; his other arm securely wrapped around his young daughter.

"Don't yell so," he said in a quiet voice. "I have you now, and I won't let you fall."

Hearing her father's subdued voice, Beverly instantly calmed down.

Chris whispered into Beverly's ear, "If you are scared, close your eyes and count very slowly to ten; then open your eyes."

Beverly closed her eyes and began counting: "One ... two ... three ... four ... five ... six ... seven ... eight ... nine ... ten." Opening her eyes, Beverly found herself at ground level. She looked and said, "I wasn't scared. I knew my daddy would rescue me."

After everyone calmed down, Janice and her family headed home. As they entered the house twenty minutes later, they looked at each other and Rodney asked, "Whew, what is that awful smell?"

Everyone started moving in different directions, following the direction they thought the smell was coming.

Walking from the kitchen, Wendy said. "Beverly, walk through the dining room. The smell is stronger in there than it is in the kitchen."

As Beverly stopped in the dining area, she pointed and said, "This is where the smell is coming from. Look at the fish—they are floating upside down."

"If the fish are upside down, they are dead," replied Rodney. Janice touched the side of the glass. Raising her eyes at Chris, she said, "The water is hot—not warm, but hot. It has changed colors. You did not leave the thermostat as you found it."

Hearing this, the children asked their mother. "Is that why our fish are dead, because the water is too hot for them?"

"Yes, my dears, the water is too hot. Children go into the backyard and did a hole under the lemon tree to bury them,"

"Wouldn't it be a lot easier to just flush them down the plumbing?" Chris asked.

"Yes, it would be easier, but I would rather they fertilize the lemon tree. Okay children, take the fish out of the tank with the nets and we will say a short prayer before burying them."

Gathering in the backyard, Rodney said to the dead fish, before shoveling dirt over them. "Daddy did not mean to cook you little fish; it was an accident."

No one else said anything. They watched the sand fall over the little bodies.

Chapter Six

Chris was tired of working at the service station. One afternoon while checking under the hood of a patron's vehicle, he said aloud, "I am tired of pumping gas and dealing with crazy people."

Getting out of the vehicle, the patron asked, "Did I hear you say you were tired of pumping gas?"

"That you did," He firmly stated.

The man walked slowly around Chris, looking him up and down. After a few minutes of inspection, asked, "Have you considered going into sales?"

"What kind of sales, furniture?"

"Selling real estate, you would have to study and pass the Florida Real Estate Commission examination (FREC). You could do it, that is, if you're really tired of filling other people's cars with gasoline." He gave Chris his business card. "Give me a call sometime."

A few days later Chris told Janice, "I'm changing jobs. I have a job with Standard Real Estate."

"What will you do there?" she inquired as she stood ironing the children's clothes for school the next day.

"I will start by answering the telephone and taking messages. Most of my time will be spent studying for the Florida real estate examination. You know I have always wanted a job pushing a pencil; now I am on my way. Once I pass the exam, I'll be on my way to becoming wealthy."

After Chris had taken the FREC exam, one minute he was positive he had passed; the next he was positive he had failed. He only needed a score of 75 percent to pass. Three weeks later he received notice that he had passed the examination and had thirty days to decide for whom he would work. He notified the board to send his license to Standard Real Estate and joyfully began his career as a real estate salesman.

On the morning of Easter Sunday, Chris said to Janice, "Let's surprise the children by taking them to Westside Park in Pompano for a picnic and an Easter egg hunt. I'll call Minnie and Tom to meet us there with their children."

The children were excited at the idea of putting on their new clothes.

"Where are we going," they kept asking. Their excitement reached an even higher pitch when they saw their father putting the ice-cream churn into the car.

At the park, they decided that the men would hide the Easter eggs and the women and children would hunt for the eggs. Some of the eggs were prize eggs. Written on the hard-boiled eggs were amounts for five cents, twenty- five cents, and one dollar. Everyone vowed to find the one-dollar prize egg.

During the middle of the egg hunt, Minnie screamed. "I've found it! I have the dollar egg!"

Wendy ran to Minnie and asked to see the egg. "This isn't the dollar egg," Wendy said, "this egg has written on it the words 'try again'." Everyone laughed and started hunting again.

Beverly walked to the chain-link fence that surrounded the baseball field. There, between the links of the fence was an egg. Lifting the egg from the fence, she saw "one dollar". Beverly was the winner.

After the egg hunt the men played a game of basketball—fathers against sons. Tom ended up with a skinned elbow and Chris with a sprained ankle.

When the basketball game was over, the families started to churn the ice cream. Janice and Minnie mixed the ingredients and readied the churn. The men churned; then the boys churned. After the handle of the churn became difficult to turn, the men challenged the ladies to see who could turn the handle more times—Minnie and Janice against Tom and Chris.

Janice was trying to turn the handle, but the whole churn moved. "Help me, Minnie," she asked.

Looking on to see how she could help, Minnie replied, "I am going to sit on top of the churn to hold it still while you turn the handle." "This did help to hold the churn still for a few turns of the handle; then, as Janice continued to turn, Minnie fell to the ground, laughing as hard as she could. The men won the contest. Chris walked to Janice, placed his arms around her, kissed her, and said, "I still love you, even though you are not Mighty Joe Young."

Returning his kiss, she replied, "You should thank your lucky stars I don't look nor smells like him."

Chapter Seven

Janice was completely happy in her marriage. Chris sometimes sent her flowers, just because he loved her. One Saint Valentine's Day, he came home with a large white box in his hands, tied with a large red ribbon. Squealing with joy, Janice kissed him and tore the ribbon from the box. Inside was a red and white dress, very pretty indeed.

"Thank you lover," she gushed. "The gift you have given me is much better than the gift I have for you."

Tearing the paper from his gift, Chris said, "I'll love it, no matter what it is, as long as it's from you." Her heart warmed at these words.

Janice smiled as she took in the smile on her husband's face as he removed the pipe and tobacco from their wrappings. There was also a glass jar for tobacco and a wooden stand to hold his pipe and the jar.

"Thank you," he said. "Maybe I will be able to cut down on my cigarette smoking."

The next evening Chris opened the front door and received the surprise of a lifetime. Standing before him, hands over her head, was Janice, completely nude except for a red ribbon draped around her body. The large bow rested at the spot where the top of her legs met.

"Happy after-Valentine's Day," she said as she grabbed him and started to remove his clothing.

"Where are the children?" he asked.

"They are at the park until we pick them up," she answered.

Later, when Chris and Janice reached the park, the children looked at them and said to each other, "They have been at it again, just look at them."

Chris and Janice were completely happy with the way their marriage was going; they were the ideal couple. Chris always made Janice feel special. Anything he thought would make her happier than she was, he would do it. The two of them laughed whenever their male friends called Chris henpecked. He always replied, "I don't mind being henpecked as long as it's by the right hen."

Their family was different from the other families in the neighborhood. Chris and Janice always took their vacation as a family, and they often went on trips alone together. There was none of this liberation attitude of, "I go where I want to go and you go where you want to go." Their family was a group made up of five people. Chris had stopped visiting bars years ago. Instead of visiting a bar on the weekend, he took his family to a movie and to dinner. Most times, if they went to the drive-in, Janice popped popcorn and carry it in a large brown bag.

Janice was exceedingly happy; she kept telling Minnie and anyone who listened that she knew her marriage was going to last forever. Chris loved her and the children more than life itself. She had no doubt in her mind. "I feel sorry for the women whose husbands run around on them and don't take time with the children."

Her friends told her not to believe life was only made up of happy times. Things are not always the way they seem, they warned, and everyone has unhappiness sometimes in their lives, married or unmarried.

"That's true," Janice replied, "but I know that Chris and I will always be together, and that we will remain happy with each other. It takes two to make a marriage and it takes two to work and keep things going. Chris and I both want the same things out of life."

Chapter Eight

Working in real estate kept Chris away from home more than usual. Janice enjoyed reading, but after a while she became tired and wanted something different to occupy her free time. After much thought, she decided to take a typing class at the adult center. In the beginning, she wondered what she would do if she ever typed a complete paragraph without errors. She was determined to learn to type, and at the end of the semester, she was ready to leave the beginner's class.

After three semesters of night classes, Janice was determined to find a typing job. Glancing at the help wanted ads in the local newspaper; she wrote the telephone numbers of businesses that did not require speed typing. It took over a month, but Janice finally landed a job, working for a typing service. She started out as a clerk typist, but after her first six months, she was promoted to proofreader.

One day Janice asked Chris, "Honey, would it bother you if I made more money than you?"

"Hell, no, if you make more money than me, it would just be more money for me to spend."

Chapter Nine

The year 1973 started out with a bang in Fort Lauderdale. All the ingredients were there for a New Year's Eve disturbance on the beach. Alcohol was definitely one of the main ingredients. Everywhere Janice and Chris looked, there were young people drinking beer and wine.

In an alcove outside the Palm Room at Las Olas and Atlantic Boulevard, a small struggle turned out to be a struggle between a hostile crowd and the police for control of the beach between Las Olas and Poinsettia. The struggle started when two police officers who were attempting to arrest a man for assaulting a girl were forced to retreat before a crowd of approximately two hundred people. Shouts of "Get the pigs, kill the pigs" were abundant. As Janice and Chris walked along the sandy beach, Chris said, "Let's get out of here before we get hurt. I want no part of this violence."

As they walked past the palm Room and the Bottoms-up Lounge, they noticed the bouncers locking the doors to keep their patrons in and newcomers out. This was being done in voluntary compliance with a police request.

There was a growing feeling of hostility in the area. Glancing over his shoulder, Chris pulled Janice along the crowded street. On Atlantic Boulevard, north of the Palm Room, projectiles were being thrown by the crowd at the police officers. A short time later, one officer noticed that the Ocean Lounge in the middle of the disturbed area was still open.

Using his loudspeaker, the officer requested that the owner of the lounge lock all his doors.

The owner of the lounge answered through his loudspeaker, "The cops said to close. There is a bad scene going on outside, the cops are out there with clubs and tear gas."

Hearing this, the patrons of the lounge were incensed and incited by the announcement; they spilled out onto the sidewalk.

By this time, the crowd had completely taken over Atlantic Boulevard. As the hostile mob moved northward, an angry man armed with a chair cracked Officer Don Bryant on the head in front of Lum's Restaurant. Other officers immediately rushed to arrest the assaulter.

As one officer tried to handcuff the offender, the offender turned his head and bit the inside left bicep of Officer Bryant quite severely. Stunned, Officer Bryant wrestled him to the ground, and with the help of two other officers, handcuffed him. It was also necessary for one of the other officers to use his club on the subject to force him to release his hold on Officer Bryant's arm. Another officer had to use his club on a person who attempted to stop the police from putting the subject in the police car, as well as on the subject's legs to stop him from kicking.

At this time, the police had lost control of the beach, and some of the members in the crowds were attempting to pull the officers into the crowd. The officers were swinging at anyone who came close. Shortly after, the officers hurled tear gas from the beach into the crowd.

At some point during the ensuing struggle, one police officer was hit over the head with a garbage can. Another officer was approached by a hippie- type motorcyclist, and the officer prepared for trouble. To the policeman's surprise, as the hippie approached, he took off his helmet and gave it to the officer, saying, "Here, you need this more than I do."

Seeing this, Chris muttered, "I don't believe it—a hippie helping an officer of the law. Now I have seen everything."

As Chris and Janice continued away from the disturbance, someone threw an object across the electric lines, shorting out the street lights. Looting quickly broke out.

When the looting started, however, police—with the help of the sheriff of Broward County's canine units—were able to arrest many of the looters. Shortly thereafter, the crowd was brought under control.

Driving home, Chris asked Janice if she missed the children, who were spending the night with his mother.

"Yes, I miss them, but I need some time away from them. Do you miss them?"

"I don't like the idea of them being away from home. If you had asked me before you took them to Mother's, I would have told you not to take them."

"Honey, you aren't with them all the time as I am," she replied. "I need some peace and quiet. They never call 'Dad'—it's always 'Momma.' I need a break."

Chris rushed into the house asking, "Baby, do you like my haircut?"

"It looks fine, now hurry. If you don't rush we'll be late."

Chris was always late for appointments and shows and Janice was always early. Tonight they were attending a Black and White Ball and were scheduled to meet Minnie and Thomas in the lobby of the Sheraton Hotel at seven-thirty for photographs to be taken before the ball. She had laid is black tuxedo and her white evening gown across the queen sized bed. She had showered, applied her make-up and the final things left was to put on her gown. He rushed into the bedroom and was ready to leave in forty minutes.

"We still have time to spare," he said as he backed from the drive.

Needless to say, traffic on east Sunrise Boulevard was bumper to bumper. Parking was a chore but they finally entered the foyer of the ballroom fifteen minutes late. Tom and Minnie were waiting.

The evening was almost perfect. They saw friends they had not seen for over a year. The two couples kept the dance floor busy. The only compliant was the cost of alcohol.

"Since integration everything has almost doubled in price," Tom complained and everyone at the table agreed.

Chapter Ten

Arriving home from work one Friday, Janice noticed the quietness of the house. Walking through the house calling the children, she heard a car in the driveway. Opening the door, she saw Chris walking toward her.

"Where are the children?" she asked.

"In Pompano," he replied. "We are spending the weekend in Key West, so I took the children to your parent's house. They don't know we are going out of town."

Happiness spread throughout Janice's heart like a ray of bright sunshine. Putting her arms around her husband's neck, she said, "Chris, I am glad we are going to spend some time alone together; we need it. Oh, honey, I love you so much!"

"I must put our bags in the car," he said. He removed her arms and walked into the bedroom.

A few hours later as they were driving on the Seven Mile Bridge, Janice said, "Thank you for packing for me. You must have really been in a hurry to get away from your heavy workload." Gazing out the window she continued. "Look out there at that beautiful water. It's so clear I can see the bottom. That spot is green, a little to the west the water looks blue, and then a little further west it begins to take on a lavender color. Just viewing the water has a calming effect on anyone that is blessed enough to gaze upon it."

That night, after getting into bed, she tried to pull Chris toward her.

"I'm tired," he said. "Let's wait until tomorrow morning—after that long drive, all I can think of is sleep."

Disappointed, she turned on her stomach and tried to sleep.

The next morning, she awoke to the sound of fishing tackle being moved around the room. Opening her eyes, she saw Chris tying a leader on the test line; then he reached for a lead ball. "Why didn't you wake me?" she inquired.

Ignoring the question, he said, "Hurry and get up. The longer you remain in bed, the less fish we'll catch."

Staring at him she said, "I'll catch a bigger fish than you, want to bet on it?"

"There is no sense in taking your money; you'll never catch a bigger fish than me," he bragged. "I am a professional fisherman. Not only will I catch the largest fish, I will also catch more fish than you. I can't let the male side of the family down; Rodney would never forgive me."

"Let's go down to breakfast," Chris continued, as he gathered the fishing gear. "I'll put the gear in the car while you dress."

Later as they were fishing from the rocks, Janice asked, "Honey, what gave you the idea of coming down here for the weekend? Was it a spur-of-the- moment idea?"

"I felt that we needed to get away for a while. We used to come here at least once a month, but somehow we seem to have gotten away from it."

"Yes, we did come down quite a lot, and we always enjoyed it. All we had to do was dial room service whenever we wanted to eat, no housework, no telephone ringing all the time—this was an excellent idea."

Sunday morning on the drive home, Janice was very quiet. Not once had they made love. She had made passes, awakened him in the morning with kisses, and still he did not make love to her. Fighting back tears, she realized she did not want to face the trouble in her marriage. 'Maybe it will work itself out,' she decided.

Chapter Eleven

One Evening as janice was finishing the dishes, the telephone rang, drying her hands on a dish towel as she walked. "Hello?" A voice she had never heard before asked, "May I speak with Mr. Blunt?"

"He is not at home, may I take a message?"

The strange voice continued, "Yes, you may. Will you tell him that miss Pat DeWitt called and would like to know if he has gotten the information about the car insurance? He was supposed to call a friend of his to let him know I was interested in purchasing car insurance. Please tell Mr. Blunt I said yes, I will get the insurance from his friend."

"Yes," Janice answered, "I will give him the message."

As she replaced the receiver, she had an unsettling premonition. The telephone call did not make sense to her. Chris was in real estate, not car insurance. She shrugged her shoulders and went back to the kitchen.

Chris arrived at nine o'clock and Janice gave him the message. He walked into the kitchen, poured himself a glass of milk, and asked, "Did she say yes?"

"Yes, she did."

Chris looked at the milk in the glass as if it were a crystal ball and smiled a secret smile. Then he lifted the glass of milk higher, looked back at Janice saying, "You know, I have had a pretty good day today. I have been trying to sell Miss DeWitt some property for a month. I promised to have a friend get in touch with her because she said she needed car insurance. I was hoping she would purchase the property I was off ering. I neither had, nor do I have, any intention of helping her get car insurance."

Later, as they settled in front of the television to watch "Good Times," Janice turned to Chris. "Honey, I have decided to see a marriage counselor, will you go with me?"

With these words, Janice began to pick nervously at her fi nger nails, using one nail to dig under another. Chris slowly turned, looked at her, and replied. "You can see whomever you want to see. I will not pay for it, nor will I go with you. If there is a problem in this marriage, you are it, not me. Don't bother me with this foolishness again."

"Chris, we have to do something. I think seeing a counselor will help." "I don't want to hear it."

"Don't yell," she said. "You will make the children think we are arguing." "Well, what would you call what we are doing?"

She looked up at him, "We are trying to have a civilize discussion."

"No, we are not. You are nagging and I am trying to watch 'Good Times'." He walked to the television and turned the volume louder.

Chapter Twelve

As she prepared for bed, Janice looked at the clock and frowned. The red, luminous numbers read eleven o'clock, and Chris was still at the office. He had been working late for the past six months and she was worried about his health. His doctor had warned him about his high blood pressure. She was also worried about his heavy drinking.

Before getting into bed she turned on the electric fan. The fan was approximately ten years old, 19 inches high and light beige in color. It matched the yellow, brown, and white décor of the master bedroom. The fan would not start. She hit it on top and still it would not start. After hitting it a few more times, she finally gave up and got into bed. She found that she was no longer sleepy and took a book from the bookshelf in the corner of the bedroom. As she settled down to read, she heard the car pull into the carport.

Glancing up as he walked through the door she said, "The fan will not work. I hit it on top as you sometimes do, but it didn't work for me."

Chris grunted as he undressed. Presently, he turned the fan on; it did not start. He hit it on top, without success. He walked out of the bedroom and reentered a few minutes later with a screwdriver.

"In as much as the fan isn't working, it won't hurt if I try to doctor it up." He took the grill off the back, turned the switch on, and used his fingers to rotate the blades. The fan still would not work. Losing his temper, he raised the fan over his head and smashed it to the floor. The on-off switch broke off and rolled around the floor. Janice suggested he leave the fan alone.

"It is old," she said. "We have gotten our money's worth out of it. It has finally burned itself out; let's put it to rest."

Banging the fan again, Chris said, "The fan will work. I will not burn up in this hot bedroom because this dumb fan doesn't want to work."

"Turn on the air-conditioner and leave the door open," Janice suggested.

"No, I don't want to turn on the air-conditioner. It is cheaper to use the fan." He lifted the fan again. This time as it hit the floor, sparks flew from it; the AM-FM clock radio on the chest of drawers went off, and the light in the bathroom went out. She started to laugh; a fuse had blown. As Chris stormed toward the utility room to replace the blown fuse, he said, "The fan is trying to burn me up by not working; now the lights are out and I can't see."

Janice called after him to unplug the fan first. She knew he would blow another fuse if he left the fan plugged into the socket. He yelled back, "Be quiet woman, you don't know anything."

A few minutes later the lights flickered on and then went out again. "Unplug the fan," he called to her.

"I can't hear you." She answered.

Yelling louder, he said, "Unplug the fan!"

"You know I'm afraid of electricity," she stated.

He yelled back, "I don't want to hear that shit. Shut up and unplug the damn fan."

Janice jumped from the bed and unplugged the fan. Immediately after telling Chris that the fan was unplugged the bathroom light and the radio came on. Straightway, she began to set the time on the clock, and reset the alarm.

As Chris re-entered the bedroom, Janice said, "This is the only thing I dislike about digital clocks—whenever the electricity goes off for a few seconds, minutes, or hours, the time always has to be reset. Honey, if you don't want to turn on the air-conditioning unit in the den why not sleep with the door open, or just sleep with the curtains open? Maybe the cool air from outside will blow in and cool you off."

Janice had taken the window screens down during the afternoon and cleaned them, but she had not replaced them properly. As a result, a mosquito flew in and bit Chris on the arm. He hit his arm and started looking for the fly swatter. Chris saw a mosquito flying near the ceiling, and jumped onto the bed, reaching up with the fly swatter. This action caused Janice to bounce in bed. She looked at him saying, "Honey, the window is open."

He did not seem to hear her. She said a little louder, "Chris, do you realize the curtains are open, the lights are on, and anyone passing can see directly into our bedroom? I don't want my business in the street."

By this time Chris was standing nude at the head of the bed—one foot on top of the dresser and the other foot on the bed—with the light on the dresser directly under his leg. "Anyone outside can look in and see everything without having to strain their eyes."

Without looking around he retorted, "Then I will have to be seen— these mosquitoes are trying to kill me."

"I feel sorry for you," she said to him. "Mosquitoes never bite me, they like warm blood and I am always cold."

"I have worked sixteen hours today, I hate hot weather, and the fan will not work, plus I am being eaten alive by mosquitoes. What is a man supposed to do?"

He eventually gave up and got into bed. Janice looked at him and began to laugh. He never used the top sheet, not even in the coldest part of winter. Now, in the middle of the summer, he pulled the sheet up to his chin. He looked as if he had just stepped out of the shower and gotten directly into bed without drying off.

Chapter Thirteen

Janice had notice that for the past few months she would spot a few days before her monthly cycle arrived. She was alarmed because her cycle was rarely early or late, every twenty-eight days, just like clockwork; that is, until the past few months. She mentally decided to make an appointment with Dr. Farquharson for a checkup to find out what could possibly be wrong.

Chris had been working for the real estate agency for approximately one year when he showed up at Janice's job and asked her to leave work early; there was something he wanted her to do.

"Why do you want me to leave early?" Janice asked, fear tying her stomach into knots. "What has happened?"

"Nothing has happened," he replied. "I just need to talk to you in private."

Realizing he was not telling her the complete truth, but knowing he would remain stubborn until they were away from her job, Janice told her supervisor that she had to take the afternoon off.

Leaving the parking lot, Chris directed the car toward Sunrise Boulevard. "Where are we going?" she asked.

"I have to see a man at a loan company," he answered.

"If that is what you have to do, why do you need me to leave my job? Something does not make sense," she said, leaning back on the seat and crossing her arms in front of her chest.

"You have to sign some papers. That's why you had to leave your job," he replied.

"Sign papers? What kind of papers, and what for? I must have missed something. Why don't you back up and fill me in on what's going on?" she requested.

"I owe the real estate agency sixteen hundred dollars and the only way I can come up with it is to get a loan from a mortgage company. I have tried and tried to think of another way to raise the money, but there is nowhere else to go."

"Chris, what are you talking about? How in the world can you owe that much money to the real estate company and if you owe that much money, what did you do with it? Where did it go?"

"I never really had that much money in my hands at one time; it is just that I used some of my clients' escrow account money when I should have placed it into the escrow account. I forgot to put it back; that's all. Now the company is talking about taking my license and bringing me up before the Department of Regulations."

"You mean you expect me to sign papers to pay back monies I have never seen nor used? In other words, you expect me to pay your client's escrow money?"

"I will get the money back. All I have to do is wait for my commissions from property sales to come in, then I will repay the loan; I'll have this loan paid off within three months," he stated.

"If that's the case, why can't the real estate agency wait the three months? I don't like the idea of a second mortgage on the house; it is not good to borrow money when it's not necessary," she replied.

Hearing this, he yelled, "Stop being hard to get along with and sign the damn papers! If I didn't have to I never would drag you into my business!"

By this time, they were in the parking lot of the mortgage company.

The manager of the mortgage company was very helpful and pleasant. As Janice listened to the manager speak, she realized that Chris had tried to get the loan without informing her, but because her name was on the warranty deed, the mortgage company refused to issue the loan without her signature.

If it wasn't for that, she thought, he would have gotten the loan without my knowledge.

It hurt her to realize Chris would do a thing like that. He seemed to have changed overnight. Surely this was not the same man she had married.

How did I miss the change in him? It must have happened gradually— so slowly that it was impossible for me to see it until now, Janice mused.

I have noticed that sometimes he seems to get upset over little things. He'll call me to watch something on television, and I stop whatever I am doing to watch that particular scene. Then go back to washing the dishes or to whatever it was I was doing. Then, when one of the children needs help with his or her homework, I stop what I'm doing to help. This makes Chris mad. It seems as if he is jealous of my interest in the children's' needs, as though he were afraid I thought their needs are more important than his needs. He is a grown man and should realize that we have time for each other after the children are in bed. If he would help me around the house, the chores would be completed earlier and I could devote more time to him. He refuses to help around the house, except for taking out the garbage. He insists that the inside of the house is my responsibility and the outside is his. The yard looks like a weed patch, and as soon as the children and I get it to look better, he takes over and it goes to pot again.

That is no reason for him not to talk to me anymore. He could have been open with me about the problems he is experiencing.

All these thoughts raced through Janice's mind as she and Chris drove home from the mortgage company.

Janice finally made an appointment with Dr. Farquharson, but she did not tell him the truth about how she had been spotting for the past few months.

After completing his examination, Dr. Farquharson asked Janice if she ever felt tired.

"No, I never feel tired," she replied. "Should I?"

"Do you ever lose all your energy when you do housework?" he continued, questioning her.

"No doctor, I feel fine. Why are you asking me these questions?"

"Your blood test shows a shortage of iron. You are anemic," he replied. "I will give you a prescription for an iron builder, and that should take care of your anemia."

Her mother called to find out what the doctor had diagnosed as her problem.

"To be honest Mom, I did not tell him. I let him think I had just come in for my yearly examination. He did tell me I was anemic and gave me a prescription."

"What do you think you pay the man for? He can only diagnose your problem through the information you give him. I insist you make another appointment and let him try to find out the reason for your spotting." Her mother demanded.

During her next appointment with Doctor Farquharson, Janice broached the subject that had been bothering her for some time.

"Doctor, I was not completely honest with you the last time I was here. "What is it?" the doctor inquired. "You should never be reluctant to tell me anything about your health."

Holding her head down Janice mumbled. "Every month I seem to have this problem."

Frowning in her direction, doctor Farquharson said, "Get on the table. I'll send the nurse in to help you get ready for a pelvic examination."

As Dr. Farquharson examined Janice, he grunted from time to time, pushing and probing at her abdomen. As the doctor completed the examination and walked toward the door, he said, over his shoulder, "Get dressed and come into my office."

Seeing the tragic look on her face, Dr. Farquharson quickly relieved her fears.

"No Janice, you do not have cancer. I can see the question in your eyes. What you do have are varicose veins on the wall of your womb. That is why you are having excessive spotting before your cycle starts every month. You also have fibroid tumors."

"Doctor, what can be done about it? I am tired of smelling as if something's crawled in there and died."

"I would suggest a partial hysterectomy. A D&C may do the job, but I don't think it will work."

"What exactly is a D&C? What do the initials mean?" Janice asked. "A D&C is a dilatation and curettage of the womb," he replied.

"I will definitely not have a hysterectomy," she said, thinking of all the stories she had heard of women who had hysterectomies and lost their husbands because of it. "I want to be a whole woman, not some freak."

"You will be no different after the surgery than you are right now, except for the fact that you will no longer have a monthly cycle and you will not be able to conceive. You have three children, and you have said on more than one occasion that you do not want any more. Nor will you be a freak after surgery. There should be no decrease in your sexual appetite. As a matter of fact, you will probably enjoy sex more because the fear of another pregnancy will have been removed. Why don't you take time to think over what I have said, or, if it would make you feel better, why don't you seek another opinion?"

Rising up from the chair, she replied, "I will get in touch with you when I have discussed this with my husband. We must decide together what will be done.

Later that same evening, Chris noticed that Janice seemed upset.

"All right, let me have the bad news. What did your doctor say to upset you?"

"You had better sit down," she said. "Make yourself a stiff drink, you will need it. While you are at it, make one for me as well."

This alone was enough to make Chris's stomach churn. "It must be bad news, you don't drink."

As he gave her the drink and sat next to her on the loveseat, Janice began to tell him of her visit to Doctor Farquharson. It took her twenty minutes of crying and talking to complete the details of her visit with the doctor.

Glancing up she said, "Honey, what are we going to do?"

At this point, Chris seemed to withdraw from her. "You do whatever you have to do. If it were my body, I would not let the doctor operate."

"If you feel that way, I will get a second opinion before deciding what will be in our best interest."

At work the next day, Janice asked around for another gynecologist. Most of her co-workers recommended Dr. McCall, who had offices on Andrews Avenue two blocks from Broward General Hospital.

That night she told Chris she had an appointment with Doctor McCall the next afternoon.

Doctor McCall was very explicit in his recommendation that Janice have the surgery. "I am 95 percent sure that a D&C will not solve your problem, I strongly recommend you have the partial hysterectomy as soon as possible."

"What do you think I should do?" she asked Chris later that evening.

"As I have said before, do whatever you want to do," he said, walking toward the door.

"Don't leave!" she cried after him. "We must decide what to do together. I don't want to make a decision without knowing how you really feel about the situation."

"Do what you have to do," he flung over his shoulder and continued walking.

Janice had seen several articles in the local newspaper about blacks having too many children, and they disturbed her. These articles helped her make up her mind as to the type of surgery she would have. Later in the evening, she told Chris she had decided to have the D&C.

"Everywhere I look there are articles written about blacks having too many children, I will not allow doctors to decide how many children I birth. Since we already have three children, both doctors must think we don't need to have anymore. Later, if the D&C does not solve the problem, I will have the hysterectomy."

The next morning, Janice called Dr. Farquharson. "We are driving to New York to visit friends for the bicentennial," she told him. "I'll call you when we get back to set a date for the surgery."

Everyone enjoyed packing for their trip. The children wanted to pack everything they owned. After Janice went through their luggage and removed half of their belongings, Wendy said, "Mom, I think it is best to have it and not need it than to need it and not have it."

"I agree with you Wendy, but I really don't think you will need two pillows, and Rodney will certainly not need this rubber snake."

After removing more unnecessary items, Janice told the children to carry the packed bags to the car, where Chris was trying to arrange the bags in some kind of order in the trunk.

Except for Chris, this was the first time any of them had traveled beyond the state of Florida. As they drove north along the Florida Turnpike, Janice heard Beverly and Rodney fighting in the back seat.

Turning, she demanded, "What is going on back there?"

Don't pay attention to them Momma," Wendy said with a smile. "Beverly is being her usual mean self."

"Momma," cried Rodney, "I told Beverly to look in the pasture at the cows, and she keeps saying they are horses, not cows. Make her stop calling the cows horses."

"They are horses," stated Beverly. "He couldn't tell a cow from a horse if it bit him on the foot."

"Beverly, you are older than our brother, stop being mean and teach him correctly. You know we have not seen any horses for the last ten miles."

Mumbling under her breath, Beverly said, "I still say that they are horses."

As Chris drove along the interstate highway in north Florida, Janice noticed the song he kept singing, "Someday We'll Be Together". He didn't sing the complete song, just a part of it.

Chris and Janice had decided to each drive in alternate states. Crossing the Florida-Georgia line, Chris pulled onto the shoulder of the road and changed places with Janice.

The further north they drove, the more the family noticed the change in the vegetation. The children exclaimed over the color of the leaves on the trees and over the size of the mountains. Never before had they seen such beauty.

"I like our beaches and our palm trees," Chris said, "but I would also enjoy seeing the changes of the seasons as well. At home we can't tell one season from another."

The sun was setting as Janice drove across the Verrazano Bridge. "Chris, I wish you would drive now; my eyes are tired," she said.

"I am scared of driving on bridges; they always seem too narrow," he replied. "I keep thinking I am going to hit the rail at the side of the bridge or an oncoming vehicle."

Looking through the windshield as they continued across the bridge, Chris shook the children and said with a smile in his voice, "Wake up, children, this is a once-in-a-lifetime sight, and I don't want you to miss seeing it."

Sitting up, the children began talking at the same time. They were excited over the beautiful vision before them. The sky was filled with blimps, airplanes, and helicopters and the choppy waters of New York Harbor were filled with thousands of private pleasure boats. As they watched, fifty-three warships of the International Navy Review passed in a stately, gun-bristling parade under the bridge and then disappeared up the Hudson River.

There were approximately 250,000 people lining East River Drive and West Side Highway. "This is a beautiful sight, but I would not want to be in a crowd like that," Chris stated. "I would be too scared of being mugged or robbed."

"From the report that came over the radio a few minutes ago, the crowd is on its 'moderately best' behavior. The New York City Police Department made a two-hour helicopter tour of the entire harbor area earlier in the evening and reported that in all areas where people were gathered to watch the flotilla, everyone was having fun. There have not been any reports of violence," Janice told him.

"I don't care what the police report said; I will not put this body among that many people—especially strangers."

"Daddy," said Rodney, "who could be any stranger than you?" The people standing five deep on the crosswalk of the Verrazano Bridge looked at the vehicle as laughter drifted toward them from the interior of the car.

Ave and Hughie King owned a three-story house in Laurelton. They also had a two-month-old daughter named Hughlette.

After putting the children to bed, the four adults talked long into the night. They made plans to visit the Statue of Liberty the next day.

On Ellis Island, Rodney Looked up and said, "I always thought the Statue was white, but she is pale green "

"Yes," replied Beverly, "and her shoes look like sneakers."

"What would you like to do first?" Ave asked the group. "Look at the displays or go to the top?"

"If I am expected to walk up stairs, we had better go up now. If I wait, I won't think of walking," Chris stated.

"Blunt, there are elevators, but the lines are so long it will take us as least forty-five minutes just to get on one—and there is no guarantee that our group will be able to go up at the same time," Hugh replied.

With this, they headed toward the stairs. "How many stairs are we going to have to climb?" Chris asked.

Hugh replied, "There are two stairways and they each have one hundred and sixty-eight steps, but by the time we reach the top you won't be tired. It seems less than one hundred and sixty-eight steps. The stairways wind around the same central column: one stairway is for ascending and the other stairway is for descending."

As they climbed up the stairway, Chris said, "I can't make it much further; I am already puffing."

"Aw, come on Daddy; don't let Mommy and Ave be better sports than you are. Talk to me—that will take your mind off the climb," Rodney said to his father.

"Rodney," Chris said, bending over with his hands on his stomach, "tell the ones ahead to either stop so I can rest or go ahead and I will meet them later. I have to catch my breath."

"I'm with you Blunt," said Ave, as she sat on the stairway next to him.

"I did not want to disappoint the children by saying anything, but I am as winded as you are."

As the small group moved to the side of the stairway to allow other tourists to pass, the tourists frowned their disapproval, but continued to push their way towards the top.

Later as they were leaving, Rodney said, "I would have liked to go all the way to her torch, but it is in need of repair and is closed off."

"We went as far as the observation platform at the top of the stairway within her head; be satisfied with that," quipped Beverly.

"That was neat," said Rodney, ignoring Beverly, "two hundred and sixty feet above sea level."

"Are you going to buy any souvenirs?" Ave asked Janice. "Yes. I could never go home without something from here."

"Then let me suggest we visit the displays first, that way our arms won't be full of anything—except Hughlette."

At this point, Hughlette held up her arms towards Janice. As Janice took her from her mother, the group headed toward the display area.

At noon the next day, Janice found herself in a crowd of thousands upon thousands of New Yorkers watching as the Royal Swedish Navy presented to the square-rigger Wavertree's home port, the South Street Seaport Museum, its long-missing bell. The city had begun to settle down from a spectacular bicentennial celebration, and the fourteen tall ships that were open to the public were a grand sight indeed.

"I like the tall ship Churchill best," said Hugh.

"I know you do," replied his wife. "It has an all-girl crew."

"I would have enjoyed touring the Fruzenshtern and Tovarisch," said Rodney, "but they would not let us aboard."

Beverly quickly replied, "That is because the Soviet Embassy closed them to the public for security reasons."

There were groups of protestors all around the area directing threats at the crew aboard the Soviet vessels. As Janice and her small group were leaving the festivities, she noticed that the crush of people trying to visit the ships was surrounded by protestors too.

"The sun is so hot we could fry an egg on the sidewalk," Ave complained to Janice, holding a souvenir program over her head for protection from the sun.

"Janice would you and the children like to sample some of the food from the vendors along the street? There are Italian ices, bagels and Lox—anything you would like." As Hughie spoke, they could hear cries of vendors. "Watermelon, twenty-five cents! Soft drinks fifty-cents!" Everyone heard and most kept walking.

"I have had a wonderful day," said Wendy. "All of my school friends will want to hear about what I did during my summer vacation."

Two weeks after returning from the Big Apple, Janice entered Broward General Hospital.

One month later, Janice realized she had made a mistake. The D&C did not solve her problem. Doubled over with cramps, she called Doctor Farquharson and told him of the piercing pain she was experiencing.

"Come into the office first thing tomorrow morning," he commanded.

Sitting across the desk from her the next morning, Doctor Farquharson said, "There are two ways of solving your problem. One, you can let me prescribe a painkiller for you. Every month during your cycle, you will have to take this medication. Two, you can let me do a partial hysterectomy. I would again suggest the surgery."

Standing up, he continued. "I'll give you a few minutes to think things over. Sit here and relax; I will check with you after I see my next patient."

After the doctor left the office, Janice began to pace up and down the room. "Taking pills will not solve my problem. I have no choice but to have the operation." She mumbled to herself. Stopping in midstride, she noticed her medical file folder lying open on the desk. Picking up a sheet of paper, she read its contents:

Operative Diagnosis: Dysfunctional bleeding and menorrhagia.

Operation: Dilatation and Curettage

Postoperative Diagnosis: Same, plus fibroid uterus.

Surgeon: Dr. John L. Farquharson.

Anesthesia: General

Estimated blood loss: 20 cc.

With the patient in the stirrups, examination under anesthesia after routine prep and drape revealed an 8 cm fibroid uterus with a large component to the right. The uterus sounded to three-and-one-half inches and the cavity was irregular. Endocervical curettage was then taken with a Meigs curette, the anterior lip of the cervix being grasped with a tenaculum. Once this was performed, the cervix was then dilated by means of Hank's dilators and a medium curette used to curette the endometrial cavity, producing about 5 ccs of blood and tissue. There were some irregularities noted in the uterine cavity, suggesting a submucous leiomyomata. The procedure was terminated. Hemostasis was good.

The patient tolerated the procedure well and left the O.R. in good condition.

This was as far as Janice was able to read, for at this point she heard Dr. Farquharson approaching as he talked to his nurse. Placing the report back into the open file, Janice rushed to sit.

Sliding to the edge of the chair she had just plopped on, Janice spoke heatedly to the doctor as he walked through the door. "I will not start popping pills. You'll have to do the surgery."

Doctor Farquharson casually asked, "When would you like to have it done? I can schedule it for early next week."

"No," she hurriedly replied, "Next week is too soon. We'll wait until school is open. That way my children will be away from home during the day and will worry a little less."

"Okay," he said, still looking at his calendar. "We will schedule surgery for the third Monday of next month."

"That's fine with me," she answered.

On the third Sunday in September, Janice entered Broward General Hospital. As the admissions nurse took her temperature, she commented that Janice had a slight fever, but said it was probably due to her being upset about entering a medical facility.

"My temperature is due to my being scared," she replied. "I was here two months ago for a D&C and woke with three nurses standing around me wondering if I was dead or alive; I can still smell the anesthesia. One nurse was standing on my left with a stethoscope, saying she could not hear a heartbeat. Two other nurses were on my right; one saying she could not get a blood-pressure reading, the other one was rubbing my right hand. Waking up to this, I told them, 'Take it from me, I am not dead.' If you had ever awakened to a scene like that, you would be scared too."

The nurse said, "I suggest you have your anesthesiologist look at your records from your last surgery so he can give you a different anesthesia."

Later, as Janice stood in a semi-private room with a roommate who was going home the next morning, she became agitated.

"I am going home," she announced to her roommate.

"You can't do that," the roommate replied. "They won't like that one bit, and they will be reluctant to readmit you. Since you do need the surgery, it is best to remain here and get it over."

"I am scared of being put to sleep," Janice answered. "If Dr. Farquharson would give me local anesthesia; I wouldn't have to go to sleep. I asked him if he would allow me to remain awake so I could watch the operation, but he said no because I ask too many questions. I'm going to call a taxi and go home. I won't have the surgery; I can live without it."

Her roommate continued to talk to her, finally convincing her to put her luggage into the closet and get into bed.

Janice was roused early the next morning by a nurse giving her a shot in her right hip. "What is that for?" she asked.

"This will make you drowsy in about an hour," the nurse told her. "Your surgery is scheduled for 7:30 a.m. In an hour an attendant will come to take you to the operating room."

In approximately one hour's time, a male attendant entered the room and requested that Janice slide from her bed to the gurney he had pushed into the room for a ride to the operating room. Half asleep and not wanting to move, she forced her sleepy body onto the long bed.

Drifting in and out of sleep as she was wheeled down the long corridors of the hospital, she was unable to care that she was on her way to surgery.

Entering the operating room, she saw a group of people standing around a room with an operating table in the middle with a large mirror in the center of the ceiling. Hearing 'beep, beep, beep," she looked to her right and saw a machine with a green dot moving across the lighted screen.

"Is that an EKG machine?" she inquired.

"Yes, it is," replied a lady dressed in green from head to foot, as were the other people in the room.

At this time, Janice felt someone playing with her left hand, which had been hanging on the other side of the gurney. Turning to the left, she saw a youngish man holding her left hand in both of his hands.

"What are you doing?" she queried.

"Just looking at our hands, you have nice hands," he replied.

Deciding he was strange, Janice looked back to her right and continued talking to the nurse about the machines around the wall. Consequently, she did not notice what the man was doing to her hand. In a few minutes she felt him tap her on the shoulder.

"May I show you something?" he asked. "Sure, what would you like me to see?"

He held up his right hand, and in it was a long, thin blue wire. "What would you say if I told you I had to put this needle in a thin vein in your hand?"

Looking at the wire, she retorted, "What would you say if I called you a liar? That thing could not go in my hand—it is too long. Plus there's the fact that I would not lie still long enough for you to insert it."

Smiling at her he then asked, "What would you say if I told you I had already inserted it into your hand?"

"I would call you a bigger liar. You could not have done it without me knowing."

Lifting her left hand for her to see, she saw her hand looked as if something had been inserted underneath the skin. Looking closer, she saw that the intern had indeed inserted the needle into her vein for the IV.

Looking surprised, Janice said, "I did not feel a thing; you are very good at your job. If I had known what you were doing, I would have been terrified."

"No," the intern said, "you would have driven me crazy asking questions. The nurses were told to keep you busy talking so you would not notice what I was doing." He then placed Styrofoam and a black rubber pad under her head; he also placed a long Styrofoam pad under her left arm. Then he connected the IV and asked Janice to slowly start counting backwards, starting from one hundred.

"How can I start counting when Dr. Farquharson is not here yet? He is the only one I want cutting on me, and I want to stay awake until he gets here."

At this time, Janice heard the double doors of the operating room swing open. Glancing over her head, she saw Dr. Farquharson walking toward her.

"Hi, Doc," She said and was asleep before she heard his greeting.

Waking and glancing around, Janice saw that she was not in the regular recovery room, but in the surgical intensive care unit. She was asleep before she could ask any questions.

Later, when she woke again, she remained still and listened to voices. "This one is awake now I'll take her down," a male voice said.

"No, don't' take that one yet; she has to stay here until she is truly conscious," the recovery room nurse replied.

Janice was asleep again before the nurse completed her sentence. She stayed in surgical intensive-care recovery until early afternoon.

The attendant come into the room at 2:15, and asked the nurse again if he could take Janice to her room. The nurse checked the chart at the end of the bed.

"If I can't go to my room now, will you please let this young man go to my room and inform my husband where I am? He will be worried."

"I am sure he knows where you are. The nursing staff will have informed him as to your whereabouts," the nurse replied, and with this she nodded her head to the attendant and the bed began to move toward the door.

Riding through the long corridors of Broward General Hospital, Janice became aware of a sharp pain in her abdomen. She bit her lip trying not to cry out.

Noticing, the attendant said, "Try to hold on until I get you into your bed. After you are all settled in, the nurse will give you a shot for the pain."

Within a few minutes, she was being wheeled into her room. As the gurney crossed the threshold, Janice heard her husband's voice.

"You had better find my wife, she has been gone since seven o'clock this morning, and you don't know where she is. Lady, you had better find my wife, and I mean now."

Mr. Blunt, you must take your feet off the bed," the floor nurse requested.

"I am not moving a damn thing until you find my wife," he yelled.

Looking at the door, the nurse replied, "Your wife is here. Now will you please remove your feet from the bed?"

As Chris stood, he asked, "Honey how do you feel? I thought they had lost you. Nobody seemed to know where you were or what had happened to you."

Opening her mouth to reply, a moan escaped her throat. After taking a long, slow breath, she told Chris she had been in a different recovery room.

"They had me in surgical intensive-care recovery. The nurse told the attendant I was apprehensive about the anesthesia and the doctor wanted me watched closely to make sure everything was all right after surgery."

"Mr. Blunt," the nurse said, "if you would kindly move, we can put your wife in bed."

"Give her a shot for the pain! Don't you hear her moaning?" he yelled at the nurse.

"She will get a shot for the pain after she has been placed in her bed, and we cannot place her in bed with you standing in the way," the nurse stated.

Looking fiercely at the nurse, Chris said in a well-modulated tone, "You will not touch her until you have given her a shot for the pain. If you try to do otherwise, I will punch you in the face. You hid her from me all morning and now you want her to suffer with this pain. Give her a shot for the pain, and I mean now!"

Fearing that the man was demented, the nurse hurriedly administered the painkiller.

Chapter Fourteen

After seven days, Janice was released from the hospital. Her mother, Mrs. Scruggs, visited every day to help during her recovery.

At times, Janice had gas pains in her lower abdomen that reminded her of labor pains. After suffering through another bout of pain, she said to her mother. "I had no idea gas could travel through the body like a living being; it tumbles like a baby and makes me feel as if I was going through childbirth again. Look at my stomach—it is so bloated that if someone stuck me with a pin I would probably explode. In addition, I never belch; it all passes from below."

"It is not quite as bad as that," replied Mr. Scruggs, looking worriedly at her daughter.

"Do you need a pain pill, or would you prefer ginger ale?"

"I will take a sip of Coca Cola," Janice replied.

At the end of six weeks, Janie was fully recovered, and returned to work feeling better than ever.

A few months after surgery, Janice noticed that sex with Chris had changed drastically. We have sex only once a week on Saturday mornings now. Before I had surgery, we had intercourse six or seven times a week, and sometimes more. Once is never enough for me, but Chris refuses to cooperate. He claims to be too tired, to have a headache, or not feel well.

Janice became very upset one night, and told him. "Damn, those are the excuses I am supposed to use! What has happened to us? We had a beautiful life together; now, everything seems to have fallen apart. Have I done something wrong? Have you found someone else? We need to talk and get whatever is in the way out into the open so it can be dealt with," she cried.

"Dear, there is nothing wrong," he insisted. "Leave it alone everything will be all right."

"Chris, does it bother you because I had a hysterectomy? Is that it? I am half a woman now and you can't handle it. Before I had the surgery you said that a friend of yours told you if I had the operation I would not be any good as a woman—I would just be an empty box. Well, if you used your head, you would realize that I am more of a woman now than I was before. The fear of getting pregnant has been removed; we can have all the fun we want without a worry in the world. No more waiting for my cycle to end, no more worrying if my cycle is late. We should be closer than ever now, yet we seem to be growing apart."

Ignoring the plea in her voice, he said, "I said to leave it alone," before walking from the room.

Standing outside the office building waiting for Chris to pick her up was getting Janice hot under the collar. Almost every day he came later and later explaining that he got hung-up with a client. She asked him to please schedule his appointments to leave time for him to take her home, then if needed, he could return to work. He did not reply to this suggestion. It embarrassed her when co-workers offered to drive her home.

It was dusk before he reached her. Stating he had fallen asleep and the children did not wake him.

After he dropped her at home stating he was going to see a client, Janice asked the children if they had eaten. When they answered no, she asked if Chris knew they were hungry.

"Daddy didn't come home," they answered. She quietly prepared their dinner.

After cleaning the kitchen Janice called her friend Louise Allen.

"I think I need to purchase myself a car. I am tired of Chris picking me up when he feels like it. It was almost dark when he picked me up today."

"If you're serious about a car my cousin Charlie who owns a garage on 31st has a '69 Volkswagen he wants to sell."

"How much does he want for it?"

"I don't know. Do you want me to ask my husband to check it out for you?"

"I sure do, tell him I need it now," she said with a laugh.

After the call, she thought about Chris's reaction when she told him. When he did come home, she was asleep and he did not wake her.

Charlie wanted eight hundred dollars for the little car. "When you get home tomorrow call and I'll take you to meet my cousin and to see the car." Louise told her.

"Thanks, Lou, talk to you tomorrow."

When Janice saw the little gray car, all she did was walk around it touching and smiling. Charlie could not stop looking at Janice.

"The car needs a valve job, that'll cost you but I don't want to sell it to you without telling you," Charlie supplied. "Get in; I want to make sure you like it. Drive around the block."

Sitting in the driver's seat Janice told him she did not know how to shift gears.

"That is no problem, this little baby can take you anywhere without you having to shift. It is an either or car. It can be shifted or not shifted."

Later that evening Janice called her father and asked for the money.

"Pop, he wanted eight hundred for it but since I'm a friend of Louise's he dropped the cost two hundred. Can you loan me six hundred? I'm not sure when I'll be able to repay you."

She was not surprised when her father said he would give her the money.

Secure she would be able to pay for the car, she told Chris that she was going to get transportation and he would no longer need to take or pick her up from work.

"We can't afford another car," he answered. She remained quiet.

Chapter Fifteen

One morning as the hands of the clock neared ten o'clock, Janice began to feel tired and decided to leave for the day. Pulling into the driveway, she noticed Chris's car under the carport. This was strange, he usually was gone during the morning hours. As she unlocked the door and entered the living room, she slowed her steps. She heard voices and movement as someone rushed around behind the closed door of the bedroom.

Hesitating, she neared the door and slowly opened it to find Chris and her neighbor from across the street standing next to the bed.

"What's going on here?" she cried.

Chris looked at her, then at Thelma, and said. "Nothing is going on. Thelma came over to use the telephone."

"Why use the telephone in my bedroom?" Janice asked, looking toward her neighbor. "Isn't your telephone working? "It was last night because Chris called and asked Carl to go fishing with him this weekend."

Replying to this, Thelma said. "Carl did not pay the telephone bill by the deadline, which was last night, and the telephone company disconnected our service this morning. I was trying to call a taxi to go pay the bill."

"Thelma, that is all well and good, but stay the hell out of my bedroom, and my house, when I am not at home. Now, let the doorknob hit you where Jesus split you."

Getting the hint, Thelma rushed from the house. After she had gone, Janice turned to Chris, "Of all the nerve! You are too tired to make love to me, but you invite my neighbor into my bed."

"Don't act crazy," he replied. "She came to use the telephone and that is all."

A few minutes later he left for work, leaving Janice with a confused look on her face.

When Janice arrived from work the next day, she knew something was different in her bedroom. The wicker wastepaper basket with a plastic trash bag to keep the ashes from Chris's cigarettes from falling through ruining the carpet was different. Normally, the plastic bag was pulled outward over the wicker, but now the plastic was folded inside the waste basket. The new breeze-box fan was sitting on top. Removing the fan, she bent and opened the garbage bag. Under the folded bag, she saw two balled-up letters. She wondered why Chris had thrown them away and tried to hide them. Smoothing out the crushed letters, she noticed that one was from the bank that held their mortgage, and the other was from the electric company.

The letter from Florida Power and Light was a final notice, and the letter from the mortgage company stated as follows: "The check has been returned due to insufficient funds. Your payment of cash, money order, or cashier's check by return mail will avoid the necessity of handing this item to our attorneys for the appropriate legal action. Since your payment was not received in a negotiable form. The total amount is due at this time in order to bring your account up to date. This is a serious matter which requires your immediate attention." At the top of the letter, stamped in large red letters, were the words CASH ONLY – NO PERSONAL CHECKS ACCEPTED.

Janice could not believe her eyes. How could the electric bill or the mortgage be in arrears when Chris cleared over three hundred dollars a week? Plus, her paycheck was faithfully deposited into their joint account every two weeks. After thinking of a million different reasons for the bills being unpaid, she talked herself into believing that the check had arrived at the bank before the deposits had been posted.

That is the reason Chris has been working very hard lately; I won't bother him about it. She decided. Everything will balance out in the end. But she continued to think about it.

As the months passed, it seemed to Janice that every time she wrote a check, it bounced due to "insufficient funds." Like clockwork, she deposited her paycheck into their account, and like clockwork the checks she wrote were returned.

At first Janice could not understand what was happening with their account, but as time passed she realized Chris was lying to her when he said that the bank had made a mistake with their accounting.

She accidentally learned the truth. Reaching home from work one afternoon her neighbor called out, "I have some of your mail; the mailman left it here by mistake."

Walking to the fence that divided their properties and accepting her mail, Janice thanked her neighbor. A few minutes later, as she sat at the dining room table flipping through the mail, she came upon the bank statement. She realized it had been a long time since she had seen one. Deciding to find out the condition of their account, she opened the envelope and started reading the cancelled checks. This is very unusual, she thought, noticing numerous cancelled checks made out to cash. Why would Chris write so many checks for fifty and one hundred dollars made out to cash? Thinking back, she remembered that Chris had stopped filling in the stubs of the checks he had written. He never so much as wrote in the amount of the checks he wrote, nor did he indicate to whom the checks were going.

Something screwy is going on, and I must think of myself now and stop being naive. I am tired of depositing my paycheck into our account and having the checks returned for "insuffi cient funds."

Th at evening Janice asked Chris why he had written checks for cash. His response was fast and furious.

"Can't I do anything without you questioning my motives? I did not feel like fi lling all that shit in, that is why. You don't need to know everything I do; now leave me alone."

His reaction devastated her. She was not used to him talking to her in that manner. Th ey had always been a close family, but lately he seemed to be changing, little by little. He must be under too much pressure on his job, she decided. In case he is getting the seven-year itch, I had better cover myself.

Janice opened a separate checking account. She did not tell Chris. If this was just a phase he was going through, she did not want him to bring this up whenever they had an argument. She also started applying for credit cards in her name at local department stores. She had worked at the same job for six years, and knew it would not be hard to get credit.

Within a few months, Janice had a number of credit cards. Now, if things continue to deteriorate, I will be able to jump from the frying pan to the counter top instead of jumping from the frying pan into the fi re. I must keep my head and never over-extend myself, she decided with pleasure.

Janice watched a commercial on television advertising contact lenses. She had worn eyeglasses since her senior year in high school.

"I'm going to check into contact lenses. I may get a pair."

"Th ey're new on the market, I suggest you wait a few years before getting rid of your eyeglasses," Chris stated.

The next day she called her optometrist who told her she was a prime candidate for the new lenses.

"Th ey cost a lot of money. What happens if I purchase them and can't wear them?"

"Since you're hesitant, and I am sure you will be able to wear them, I'll do this. If by some reason you can't wear contacts, I'll refund all your money except the cost of the exam. How does that sound?"

"Great! When can I come in?"

When she went for her appointment, Chris went with her. He was not a good candidate for contact lenses.

Two weeks later Janice went home with new contacts. When she reached home, the children liked her new look. When Chris came home he complained and said, "You look crossed-eyed without your eyeglasses."

"You only say that because your eyes are too sensitive and contacts bother you," she countered.

The next morning she wore her new contacts to work. Her instructions were to wear the contacts for two hours the first day, three hours the next day and on until she could wear them all day. The evening of the first day she called her doctor and asked, "What happens if I wore my contacts all day?"

"Nothing, most people have to build up a callus on the inside of the eyelid and that takes time. Why do you ask?"

"Because it felt so good to be able to see clearly without a pair of eyeglasses on my face that I kept the contacts in all day."

Chris had never liked answering the telephone, but lately he seemed to be stationed next to it every time it rang. If one of the children was near when it rang, he yelled at them to let it ring more than once before they answered.

"What's wrong with you, Daddy?" Beverly asked. "You've always told us to answer the telephone as soon as it begins to ring because you hate to hear the ringing sound. Now you jump down our throats if we answer on the first ring. I wish you would make up your mind."

"Someone seems to be playing games with us anyway," interjected Rodney. "Sometimes I answer the telephone and the person on the other end won't say anything."

Listening to this conversation, Janice began to feel uneasy. The same thing had been happening to her lately, but she had put it off as a prank. Now she began to wonder who could be behind those calls. Chris seemed more interested in answering the telephone himself. And, whenever he answered, whoever was on the other end of the line would always talk; the person also seemed to be a friend with an unfamiliar name to Janice. It was strange that no one ever seemed to hang up on him.

I hope my fears are unwarranted. I don't know what I'll do if our marriage falls apart. Chris and the children are my life; there is nothing else for me.

Not long afterwards, Janice got into bed, but she wanted to do something to keep her mind busy. Reaching for the telephone on the night stand next to the bed, she called Louse.

"How are you Lou?" she asked.

"I'm fine, Janice," came Louise's voice.

"Lou, I have been thinking. I am bored with working every day and staying home every night. I passed a ceramics shop this afternoon and a sign in the window said classes were being offered and to just come in and ask about taking ceramic lessons. Would you be interested in attending classes with me?"

Louise's voice came over the telephone loud and clear. "Yes, I would. I have always wanted to take ceramic lessons but I never had anyone to go with me."

"Good, what time do you finish your housework?"

"I finish around six o'clock," Louise answered.

"Fine, I'll pick you up at six-thirty tomorrow evening."

Janice felt somewhat better. A ceramics class would get her out of the house a few nights a week and would also keep her mind busy.

The next evening, Janice picked Louise up at the appointed time.

Louise was reddish-brown in color, five feet four inches tall, and weighed approximately one hundred thirty pounds.

As they drove south along Northwest 31 Avenue, Louise asked Janice what had given her the idea of taking ceramic lessons.

"I have been thinking of different things I could do to keep busy. Since Chris works so late at the office, I considered going back to school and taking night classes, but decided against it because Chris got bent out of shape about me going to night school when I took typing and shorthand. I don't think he will argue about ceramics; it is not the same as book learning."

"In addition to his raising hell about me going to school, we were visiting Minnie and Tom in Pompano, and Tom asked a question that Chris did not know the answer. Without thinking, I answered the question. Chris said so everyone could hear, 'I hate a smart-assed woman.' Minnie looked at me and said, "Janice, I think Chris is jealous of your education."

"I think you are right Minnie," I replied.

"Although I only have a high-school education, I have taken additional courses at night. Chris feels bad because he dropped out of high school his senior year. It has always bothered him, but he won't do anything about it. I have tried to encourage him to attend night classes. I think he feels he would be ridiculed by our friends. I have told him that by going back to school, he could influence someone else to go back."

As Janice turned right on Davie Boulevard, she said over the loud motor of her Volkswagen, "Like it or not, Chris is always working and I refuse to remain home every night. Going to ceramics class is better than going to the bars around here."

A few weeks later, Janice was getting ready to paint a vase she had been working on, she asked Louise if she had any suggestions as to the colors she should use on the vase.

"Paint it in your favorite colors," Louise answered.

Janice leaned her head toward her right shoulder, looked at the vase while turning it, and said, "I think I'll paint the vase yellow and white, and the little boys flesh color."

When she asked the instructor for the paint, her instructor suggested she use her light colors first and darker color last. That way, if Janice came too far with the lighter colors, the dark paint would cover the errors made with the lighter colors. Janice looked at the jars of paint Helen placed on the work table, "I did not ask for this pink paint. I want flesh-colored paint."

Helen looked at Janice and said, "That is flesh-colored paint."

Janice looked directly into Helen's eyes and said, "I mean my flesh color, brown. I don't mean to put you down, but any time I paint people they will always be brown: light, medium or dark brown."

Helen turned a bright shade of red. "I'm sorry. I never thought of flesh being any color except pink. I'll get your brown right away."

Janice turned to Louise. "I can buy white-people ceramics from any store. The only black ceramics I have ever seen are the black Sambos standing next to driveways holding lanterns so that passers-by can see the name of the family or the address of the people who live there. I intend to give my pottery as Christmas presents this year; they will be distinctive and attractive."

During one class, Janice was painting a pair of Chinese statues. A new member of the class was sitting across from her. "Why are you painting the Chinese with brown skin? Their skin should be yellow."

Janice replied, "Every object I paint will have people with brown skin. How do you know there are no black Chinese people? Blacks have the opportunity to travel just as other races do; however, we may not travel as often and fewer blacks travel that far, but some of us manage to travel to foreign countries."

As a result, ceramics class was therapy for Janice; it gave her something to occupy her mind while Chris worked. Furthermore, she had started bringing projects home to paint.

Chapter Sixteen

It was very late when Chris came home, supposedly from the office. Janice was in bed reading. As Chris began to undress in the bathroom, she asked where he had gone after he left the office. He mumbled. She asked him what he had said and he mumbled again. The third time she asked him and he mumbled, she remained quiet. She waited until he was in bed before asking again where he had gone after he left the office. Pretending to be asleep, he did not say a word.

Leaning over she spoke into his ear, "If you don't answer me, I'll punch you in the side. I know you are not asleep; I also know you left the office early."

Turning to face her, he said. "I went to Richard Dupree's house."

"Thank you. I did not know you had left the office early. I took a chance to see what your answer would be."

"I am tired and want to sleep," he replied as he pulled the cover to his chin.

Fuming, she said, "I don't give a damn about you being tired. I am sick and tired of you spending six nights a week at the office. When you go somewhere, you go directly from the office without thinking about me; I would like to accompany you sometimes. All you have to do is call when you are ready to leave the office and I can be dressed and waiting by the time you get here."

Taking a deep breath she continued. "We still have sex only once a week. You keep telling me you are thirty-eight years old and your body has changed. Well, my body is thirty-six years young, and it has not changed; it still wants to be made love to. Also, we don't have any friends. You are always working, so our friends are tired of coming here because you are never home. We owe everyone a visit."

Speaking in a calm voice, he replied, "Why don't you return their visit? That's somewhere for you to go."

"Don't use that well modulated tone of voice on me, you sanctimonious bastard," she yelled, and slapped him across the face.

He sat up and grabbed both her wrists. "If you hit me again, I will knock you out."

Janice pulled her right hand free and slapped him again. "If you hit me I won't feel any worse than I already feel."

He stared at her for a long time. Finally, he turned his back and went to sleep.

The next evening when Chris arrived from work, Janice was sitting on the love seat in the den reading the newspaper. As he sat next to her, she moved without looking from her newspaper. She could see him looking at her from the corner of her eye, and wondered what would happen next. Chris continued to stare at her for over an hour.

Later, as he was putting change on the table for the children's lunch the next day, he asked if she had change for a dollar.

"I have less than a nickel," she answered.

When they went to bed, Chris lay so close to Janice their bodies touched. She moved away from him; she did not want him touching her. Throughout the night, he kept moving toward her in bed. At one time, his rear end was on her back, and he would not move as she punched at him. She turned, took her hands and pushed his rear end back onto his side of the mattress. She awoke at five-thirty and realized that Chris was also awake. He left the bed for the kitchen putting on a pot of coffee, then climbed back into the bed, lighting a cigarette. After the cigarette had been smoked, he lay with his feet and buttocks touching her. She moved to the very edge of the bed to the rim of the mattress. Six o'clock the alarm rang and she dressed and left for work.

Three days had passed since Janice had slapped Chris and they were still not speaking. The only words spoken between them were when the children were present. Janice agonized in her mind. He is treating me as if I were the one who is always gone. Last month, on his only night off, he had left home around five o'clock to visit a co-worker he always said he disliked. He called home at eight to say he and his co-worker were going to J.W.'s on University Drive for a drink. Why couldn't he take me with him?" she wondered.

That same evening, Rodney had came home at eight-thirty, looked at her frowning and stated, "Momma, I thought you were with Daddy."

"No," she replied. "He has gone to visit a co-worker."

Rodney said, "I saw Daddy driving on 31 Avenue with a lady in the car around five o'clock. I thought it was you in the car with him."

Looking at her son, she said. "You must have seen the headrest and mistaken it for me."

Later, she kept wondering if she should mention this incident to Chris. If it was true, she did not know how she would handle it. At length, she decided to let it rest and not mention it.

Four days later, Janice could stand it no longer. She turned off the television and went into the bedroom where Chris as polishing his shoes.

Janice was worried she was losing Chris. He is fooling around on me, but if I continue to turn away from him when he wants to have intercourse, he will use that as a excuse for our failing sex life. It will be my fault. I will swallow my pride and try to bring us closer.

"Chris, it has been nine days since we made love. If I want sexual release, I have to use my vibrator or some other substitute. Doesn't it embarrass you that your wife has to use a tool for sexual release? In addition, the vibrator hurts the bottom of my stomach."

He glanced up, and then continued brushing his shoes, saying nothing.

She stormed at him, "If I could afford it, I would damn sure get rid of you. I get tired of you never having any money when the children need something for school. Wendy will be going on a trip with her classmates next month and you didn't have the money for it. I had to borrow the money from my mother. Wendy is a senior and needed pictures taken for the yearbook, but you could not come up with eight dollars. It is amazing how you never have any money, but still manage to play cards every Thursday night with your co-workers, go to J.W.'s, and keep a steady supply of liquor and cigarettes."

He continued brushing his shoes as she stomped her foot again and left the room.

Janice decided to do some serious thinking about her marriage. I cannot ignore the problem any longer. Chris and I have too many years invested in each other to just let it go without trying to do something to salvage it. I am going to insist that we sit down and discuss this fully. We need to talk openly and honestly about all things that are bothering us—talk them over and try to work the problems out. If we don't begin to work on the problems now, it will continue to get worse, until there will be no hope of them getting better.

The past year has been pretty bad, she thought, compared to the previous years. We no longer have the intimate relationship we once had. Sex seven times a week or more was the normal way of things before I had the operation. Chris must consider me a half a woman; since the surgery, it seems that something in him won't let him touch me any more than he absolutely has to. Maybe he has a girl friend and enjoys having sexual intercourse with her more than he does with me. Whatever the reason, we need to talk it out. We must be honest with each other if we are to have any kind of marriage.

The more she thought about the change in her marriage during the last year, the more convinced she became that Chris did have a girlfriend. Sometimes she called the office and no one answered. When Chris came home, she asked where he had been and he replied, "At the office."

"I called the office and did not get an answer."

"The telephones are not working properly," he answered.

Sometimes he called, ask her to warm the dinner he had missed. Tell her he would be home in a few minutes. It would be hours before he arrived.

"What happened, Chris? The food is over done now."

"I went out for a while," he answered.

"Why didn't you call me to go with you? You know I get tired of being stuck in the house all the time."

To this she received no answer. Chris could never stand being at home without Janice, but he continued to leave the office and go places without asking if she would like to go with him.

Thinking back, Janice remembered she and Chris had taken their vacations together, but he had spent most of the time elsewhere, leaving her to wait for him to come home.

When Chris and Janice married, they both agree that if either of them found someone they wanted to go to bed with, they would talk to each other first. They both wanted openness and honesty in their marriage. Chris had found someone and had not bothered to tell her; actions speak louder than words, and his actions could not be plainer. They were both home on weekends, did not have to rush around for any reason, and yet they did not enjoy each other intimately. She had to remain in bed and act as if she were never going to get dressed before he turned to her. If she happened to go to the bathroom for any reason, when she returned to the bedroom, Chris would be dressed and in the den with the children, watching Saturday morning cartoons.

Within the past year, Janice's body had cried out for release, but to no avail. Sometimes she completely forgot about sex. She was getting to a point where she did not care about it; she did not care if Chris touched her or ignored her. I am too young for my body to stop wanting sex, but what do I do about it? Chris never had to worry about her being with another man—one cold-hearted man was enough.

Chris did not seem to be able to mix business with pleasure, at least not where his family was concerned. Janice was just someone to cook for him, clean for him, have his children for him, and keep his children from running wild in the street.

Janice wanted Chris to think seriously about what he wanted out of life. He could not continue both his job at the real estate agency and the night life he was leading, coming home at one o'clock or later.

"I want to get ahead," he would reply to her question.

"If getting ahead means going on in this manner, we will not make it together unless we go our separate ways," she flung back at him.

Chapter Seventeen

J anice stood at the door of the master bedroom taking in the brightly decorated room. It was decorated in white, yellow, and brown. She noted its clean and orderly appearance. She looked at the wicker wastepaper basket immediately to her right just to the right of the wastepaper basket was a nine-drawer gold and white dresser with a large mirror on top, trimmed in gold and white wood. Above the mirror on the yellow painted wall was a picture of Jesus, smiling. Next to the dresser, a dark brown bookcase stood, filled with rows and rows of books. Immediately in front of the dresser and bookcase was a large queen-size bed covered with a gold, quilted bedspread. At the head of the bed, sitting between the two pillows with its back resting on the gold and white wooden-framed headboard was a beige and brown teddy bear, and to the left of the bed stood a gold and white night table. On top of the night table was a white telephone, a white lamp with a yellow-and-white-checkered shade, and an AM-FM stereo radio with the time showing in glowing red light. The front of the night table had two drawers with carving. To the foot of the bed was a five-drawer chest of drawers also trimmed in gold and white; Resting on top of the chest of drawers, Janice could see an open Bible, a three-drawer white jewelry box, and a yellow candle in a glass with a gold, green, red and white butterfly pained on the side. Next to the candle, Janice could see a four-volume set of *Black American Pictorial History* books. Above the chest of drawers on the wall were two gold sconces with gold globes over white candles. Next to the chest of drawers to the right was a door that led to the master bath and to the left was a door that opened into a walk-in closet. As Janice looked at the room, she noticed the draperies hanging on the north and west walls; they were yellow, white, and brown, designed to look like bamboo sticks. Across the top hung a gold, draped valance with buttons interspaced to hold the drape in place. To complete the room, the floor was covered with yellow, gold, and white shag carpeting.

The room struck one as being a peaceful room, inviting one to rest. But looks are deceitful, for there was only turmoil and unhappiness to be found in this room.

For the sake of our children, Janice promised herself, I am going to do my best to bring a happy feeling into this bedroom again.

Not long afterwards, Chris arrived home home. "How was your day dear?" Janice asked.

"Fine," he replied. "What are we having for supper?"

"We are having Barbeque rib dinners from Chuck's Double-O-Soul Takeout."

"Chuck's Double-O-Soul? Where is that?"

"On the corner of Sistrunk Boulevard and Twenty-Second Road," she replied. "Wendy and I stopped there for lunch last week, and their food is tops in my book. You will enjoy eating there. As soon as you shower and change, we can go."

Driving away after dinner, he said, "That was a very good meal. I wonder why I have never heard of that place before."

"Let's ride along the beach before going home."

He did not complain, but drove north along Twenty-Second Road until they reached Sunrise Boulevard. Turning east, he said as they neared I-95, "This will be a sort drive; I still have work to do at the office."

Janice said, "Chris, don't you think you are driving yourself too hard?

Take the night off and let's spend some time together. We never see each other anymore. I love you and want to spend more time with you. We need to talk. Things are not the same between us." She continued in a halting voice. "Please tell me what went wrong."

"Nothing is wrong and there is nothing to talk about."

"I guess you think of me being half a woman—that is why you don't touch me anymore than you have to. Have you found someone you like having sex with better than me? Whatever we do we must be honest with each other if we are to have any kind of marriage."

Chris continued to drive along Sunrise Boulevard, looking at the stores with their lights on, all doing what seemed to be a very brisk business. As he looked to his left, he viewed a large brightly painted billboard that seemed to scream out to him, "Unwind …. Relax …. Get in tune with nature …. FORT LAUDERDALE …. Come to the waterways … the sun … the sandy beaches…. THE VENICE OF AMERICA …." In the corner of the billboard was a picture of a smiling young black woman, complete enjoyment written on her face, happiness radiating from her.

Inevitably, Janice started to cry. "You have already tuned me out! You are not listening to me. I am worried about our marriage; we have lost our closeness. What can we do to get it back?"

He turned toward her and said, "Will you stop your nagging? I spend my time away from home trying to earn a living for you and the children and you show your appreciation by being a fishwife."

"Chris, stop lying. You don't spend your time away from home at the office. I have called there time and time again and no one answers the telephone. On the other hand, I sometimes call and one of the agents tells me you have left for the day. You have changed; take last night, for example. You called around seven o'clock and asked what I had cooked for supper. 'Pork Chops', I said. Then you asked me to warm them up and you would be home soon. Half hour later your brother called and left a message for you to call him; it was an emergency. I told him you would be home any minute and I'd have you return his call. When you did not come home, I called the office to give you the message, but there was no answer. I called again at nine-thirty but to no avail. I decided your brother must have reached you and that you went to meet him. You did not think enough of me to let me know your plans had changed. Did it ever cross your mind that I get tired of staying home seven nights a week with just the children? Naturally, you cannot stand being home without me, but it is indeed certain that you continue to leave the office and go places without asking if I would like to go with you. For example, we took our vacation to be together and you spent most of it away from our room, with me stranded in the hotel waiting for you to come back."

Cursing under his breath he looked into her face and asked, "Janice, what is it you want? You are never satisfied."

"I want honesty; we said that we would be honest with each other if we found someone we wanted to sleep with. If you have found someone, you have not bothered to tell me, although your actions could not be plainer. We are both home on weekends, with no reason to rush out of bed and you still won't touch me. I have to stay in bed and keep touching you and asking you before you make love to me. Chris if we don't use it, we will lose it and I don't want to lose that beautiful feeling."

At this point, Chris turned the car north along A-1-A, heading for Oakland Park Boulevard.

"Look at that," he said, "we sure have plenty of snowbirds down here; the tourist season is in full swing. I'll bet you anything that Birch State Park closes early every day due to the park being full to capacity."

"Our marriage is at stake and you are concerned about the park being closed! I am speechless!"

"You are anything but; please continue with your dissertation."

"All right, I will. "Obviously, you cannot mix business with pleasure—

at least not where I am concerned. I wish you would seriously consider what you want out of life. You cannot have that job and continue to lead the life you are now leading without something falling apart.

"For instance, you came home at one o'clock this morning. I asked you what had happened after you had called asking me to warm your supper. You replied that you got so involved with your work you forgot the time; it was 12:45 in the morning when you just happened to glance at your watch."

Chris turned the car westward when they reached Oakland Park Boulevard. As they crossed the intra-coastal, the Paddlewheel Queen Cruising Supper Club was approaching the bridge. The bell began to clang as they started on the downward side of the bridge.

"Naturally, you won't tell the truth, she continued. "I doubt you would recognize the truth if it bit you on the lip. I called the office and got no answer. You say the telephone is out of order. It is awfully strange that whenever I call and don't get an answer, you say the telephone must be out of order, but if someone else is there, the telephone is answered and you are not there. You told me you wanted to get ahead. Honey, if getting ahead means going on this way, we won't make it together unless you go your way and I go mine. The only thing is, I don't want us to have separate lives. I was hoping my ceramics class would fill the void, but it does not."

Chapter Eighteen

Never a person to wear makeup, Janice decided to go to a department store at the Lauderhill Mall to have the saleslady show her how to apply makeup and to help her with all she would need to know to help make a new person of herself.

Reaching the mall Janice noticed the parking lot seemed extra full. A few minutes later, she realized the department store she was going to was fuller than the other stores in the mall. Forcing her way through the rows of ladies she saw a large sign at the entrance offering free makeup lessons from a well- known cosmetics firm. God must be on my side, this is exactly what I need.

An hour later, after spending more than fifty dollars, Janice left the store feeling good. The makeup lady had the exact combination of makeup. Janice looked like a new person and the makeup helped Janice feel more confident.

Now Chris will see the person I can be. This will make him stop running around with other women, she thought.

A week had come and gone, and Chris did not seem to notice Janie was wearing makeup. It seemed to her he did not take time to really look at her, he just talked in her general direction.

"I know what to do," she said one evening to the children. "I will have my hair weaved."

Three days later, Janice came home with shoulder-length hair. She had gone to her hairdresser during her morning work hours. Everyone at work loved the way she looked.

"It makes you look younger, not that you looked old or anything," one co- worker said, making her smile.

"I love it, Momma," Wendy said when Janice walked into the house after work.

"So do we," said Beverly and Rodney as they come out of the den.

This change did cause Chris to notice, but his reaction was totally unexpected. When he walked in later that same evening, Janice was in the kitchen, standing at the stove cooking.

"What the hell have you done to yourself?" Chris asked as he stood in the doorway between the dining room and the kitchen. "The other day you came in here with all kind of shit on your face. Now, you've gone and bought a damn wig." Reaching for it, he tried to pull it from her head.

"Ouch! That hurts," she said. "It doesn't come off; it is sewed onto my own hair, STOP!"

"You are hurting me," she stated, trying to remove his hand from her now tangled hair.

"You look like a whore," he heatedly said. "I don't like the hair, and I don't like that shit on your face." With this he slammed out of the house.

Looking at the children and trying not to cry, she said, "Go wash your hands; dinner is ready."

Chapter Nineteen

The telephone on janice's desk rang. Lifting the receiver she heard the excited voice of the switchboard operator saying, "Come up front and look out the window. It's snowing! I can't believe it, but it is snowing in Florida?"

Rushing toward the front of the office, Janice told everyone she passed in the hallway, "Come see the snow! Our liquid sunshine has crystallized and it is snowing! Can you believe it?"

Entering the lobby, another co-worker glanced her way and said, "Is this Florida? Step into my cooler and warm up."

"Hurry, hurry, it is snowing!" Janice exclaimed. "But it is disappearing as soon as it touches anything." Glancing around, she saw other co-workers looking in wide-eyed fascination. One co-worker said, "I left New York because of the snow, and I'll be damned if it didn't follow me south. I'll have to move farther south."

Another co-worker quipped, "You'll have to go to South America at least. The announcer on the radio just said it is snowing in Freeport as well as here."

"I have an idea," Josephine, the switchboard operator said, "We should call Southern Sanitation Service; they offer free snow removal. I'm sure they never expected it to snow in southern Florida." Dialing the telephone, "I hope they are in good humor over at the sanitation office." She replaced the receiver a few minute later saying, "The man answering said, 'Free snow removal means we will cart it away if it has been collected in a receptacle.' He said that they have been telling callers they will try to get a truck out sometime this afternoon." Everyone laughed and went back to work.

Chris was home with the flu and slept all day without turning on the radio or the television; thus, he did not know it was snowing outside.

Excited as the children were about seeing snow for the first time, they knew to keep quiet upon arriving home from school. As a result, when Janice arrived home, the children were in their rooms, still too excited to eat, and Chris was still asleep. Deciding to take a short nap,, she was in a deep sleep when Chris awoke and went into the den to watch television. Turning the television set on, he sat back and put his feet on the black-leather love seat and relaxed.

Chris could not believe his ears when he heard the announcer speak. "For the first time since it began keeping records in 1890, the National Weather Service in Miami today issued a snow bulletin for Fort Lauderdale and vicinity. Forecasters predicted cold weather tonight, with temperatures in outlying areas of Broward County expected to be about 25 degrees."

"Honey, kids, come listen to this weather report! The news man is talking about the snow that fell today," Chris yelled at the top of his voice as he started at the television screen.

"Snow fell in Fort Lauderdale today for the first time in recorded history," the reporter announced, "with temperatures expected to plunge to 25 degrees tonight."

Janice walked into the den yawning asking, "What did you say dear?" "Listen to this special weather report."

"Flurries of snow were reported throughout Broward County this morning and it snowed even heavier in Palm Beach County. The official low temperature for Broward County was 36 degrees."

At this point, the children ran into the den from their bedrooms and sat on the floor.

The announcer continued. "According to the U.S. Weather Service, it was colder here today than in Anchorage, Alaska. Some schools in the Broward County area, the Everglades area, and in the West Palm Beach area discontinued classes due to the lack of heating, and parents were called to pick up their children. By noon today, temperatures had edged up to around 40 degrees in most of the county, but the wind, coming from the northwest, also had increased, gusting at more than thirty miles per hour. At the Fort Lauderdale-Hollywood International Airport, the temperature was 41 degrees at noon, with winds hitting at forty mile per hour.

"The strong winds will continue into tomorrow, according to the National Hurricane Center in Miami, and it is predicted that temperatures will drop in Broward County to 25 degrees inland and 30 degrees along the coast. A twenty-five degree temperature tomorrow would produce a 'chill factor' of minus seven degrees. The real low temperatures haven't gotten here yet, and I'm afraid it's going to be pretty bad tomorrow."

"I hope it snows enough tomorrow to build a snowman or to have a snowball fight," Rodney said. "We could have a really good time."

At this point, the camera switched to a reporter at a local Florida Power and Light office (FP&L). "FP&L announced that its plants had hit peak usage at seven-thirty this morning and, if the demand for power grows much heavier, it might have to ask its large commercial users to close down for the duration of the cold spell. The unprecedented demand for electricity caused breakdowns in generating plants in several areas, dropping the company's ability to produce power and leaving no reserve capacity."

Turning to the FP&L representative, the announcer asked, "What do you have to say about this unusual situation we are experiencing?"

"If those two plants cannot be put back in operation today, and if the utility has another breakdown somewhere, the situation will be critical. Residents are asked to turn their thermostats down to 68 degrees, turn off any luxury appliances and confine gas usage to warming and cooking food. The situation promises to become worse." The forecaster in Miami added, "The really cold temperatures haven't gotten here yet."

"Thank you," the announcer said. "And now, back to our local station."

The announcer back at the station continued, "No snow has been forecasted for tomorrow. The Weather Service issued a forecast for today of rain mixed with light snow. Snow flurries were reported in practically every city in Broward County, both along the beaches and inland. Heavier snow fell in West Palm Beach and Boca Raton. In the Loxahatchee area, grove owners said the snow was blowing through the fields like a blizzard. There was about a half-inch of snow on the grown through the groves."

"The children of South Florida, many of whom have never seen snow before, frolicked in the white powder. Farmers of Broward County were just about resigned to one of the biggest crop losses in history."

"Last night, those farmers got an unexpected break as a light rain fell, and this morning's cloud cover provide some protection for their tender young crops of beans, squash, cabbage, and cucumbers. However, one more night of this cold and the crops will be a total loss. The potential crop loss in Broward and Southern Palm Beach counties may exceed four million dollars.

"City dwellers were having their own problems as they struggled with the unusual cold spell.

"All the traffic signals went out on State Road Seven, north of Oakland Park Boulevard. The Salvation Army, which normally gets about twelve requests for welfare assistance per day in Fort Lauderdale, received countless pleas from the homeless and those who had fallen in arrears on their electric bills and needed the power turned back on."

"But if it was bad in Fort Lauderdale, it was far worse in other sections of Florida. A rush of traffic accidents on icy roads in the Tampa Bay area this morning left one person dead and about sixty injured. The lower Keys also experienced coastal flooding as the strong Northwest winds caused tides to rise up to two feet above normal."

"It was the snow, especially in South Florida that caught most people by surprise. The switchboard of the Fort Lauderdale News lit up like a Christmas tree as residents from all over the area called in to report snow falling in their neighborhoods."

"At Fort Lauderdale's Holiday Park, on Sunrise Boulevard, a few employees decided to hold a tennis match. 'The balls were hard and they wouldn't bounce,' the employee at the tennis center said. "I just had to play, though; I may never get another chance to play tennis in the snow.'

"Firemen in the City of Oakland Park tried to shape a snowman, but they finally gave up on the natural stuff and built one out of shaved ice from an ice-maker. "It just seemed appropriate," the fireman said.

"An employee of an equipment company in Hollywood saw the snow as a rare opportunity to get rid of an odd piece of equipment that had been around the shop for months. It was a snow thrower a customer had ordered, hoping to use it for moving sewage sludge, but he changed his mind before picking it up. It's a nice one, a John Deere."

Chris asked Janice, "What will today's snowfall do to Fort Lauderdale's image as a wintertime tropical haven for northern snowbirds?"

"The city's chief image-maker, the Greater Fort Lauderdale Chamber of Commerce, doesn't know, but the executive vice president did not seem to be worried about it. He was on an earlier broadcast on WRBD Radio and said that he didn't know how in the hell we cold capitalize on the snow, but guaranteed we would turn it into a positive event."

Janice continued, "You really must have felt awful to have slept through all this excitement today. I would have called you but I knew you had already experienced snow during your stint in Uncle Sam's Army."

Smiling at her he replied, "I know I can expect to see you climb into bed with your pajamas with the feet in them."

"Sweetheart, you are 100 percent correct on that point. The houses in South Florida are not built to withstand this cold, and the reverse cycle air conditioner we had installed in the den could never warm me enough to be comfortable. I intend to dress up when I go to bed."

It was a family joke that she always slept in a long, flannel gown with red wool socks or in her pajamas with the feet enclosed whenever the weather turned cold.

A few weeks later as Janice was trying to cook dinner, another burner on the stove refused to heat. "Honey, before you go back to the office, will you check the stove? Two of the smaller burners have stopped working, and as you already know, the larger burner stopped working last week."

"I don't have time now," he replied. "I'm already late."

"Chris, do you realize how long it takes me to cook with only one small burner usable?"

"Stop nagging, I'm going to work." He tied his tie, grabbed his briefcase and headed for the door. Stopping before walking out, he snapped at her, "Use the oven."

"How can I?" she yelled back, "both elements stopped working months ago, and you know it. You used to do this type of work; now, since you've become a real estate salesman, pushing nothing heavier than a pencil, you are too good to get a little grease on your hands. If you don't repair this stove, I am going to buy another one. You keep telling me you are going to repair it. This whole damn stove need to be thrown out."

"Okay, okay," he said holding up his hand. "I'll fix the damn thing this weekend. You are so damn headstrong and independent I am dumbfounded that you haven't already bought a new one."

Three weeks later, nothing with the stove had changed. Chris was watching a football game when Janice asked him to measure the stove for her. She was going to purchase a new one and wanted the same size.

"I told you I would fix the damn thing. I'll get to it," he insisted.

"No thanks. I would rather not wait for you to repair it. After thinking the matter over, it would be cheaper all around to get a new stove with a warranty. You told me that it costs forty dollars for each element and forty dollars for each burner; that is almost two hundred dollars. We can get a new stove for the same amount."

"For once you are making some sense. Where are you going to get the stove?"

"I am going to an appliance store on 441. Come with me; you know more about appliances than I do. I don't want a self-cleaning one; they seem to be more trouble than they are worth," She stated.

He surprised her by going with her. The stove was delivered at the end of the week, and Chris promised to install it before the weekend ended. Needless to say, a month later, the stove had not been installed. It was still in the box in the utility room. Thanksgiving was two weeks away. When Janice shopped for Thanksgiving, she did not purchase a turkey.

"I am not cooking a turkey this year. You don't deserve a turkey, you are a turkey," she said to him after returning from Public.

"I want a turkey and a ham for dinner. We have always had turkey and ham on Thanksgiving, plus all the cakes and pies you bake. I am going to install the stove as soon as this game is over."

When the game was over, he dressed and said. "Baby, I have to go out for a while. I won't be gone for more than an hour."

"Yes, Chris, I know how long you will be gone." She replied.

Chapter Twenty

The day before thanksgiving, Chris decided to install the stove. After completing the installation he said, "Your stove is installed and ready for the turkey."

"As I have repeatedly told you, I am not cooking a bird this year. If you want one, you can buy it and cook it yourself. I have been without a decent stove for months. Now, since you want a turkey, you have made it possible for me to cook. This is my holiday out of the kitchen; I am not cooking." Saying this, she continued reading her book.

What are you going to give the children for dinner?" he inquired.

"I am taking them to Pompano. My mother is having smoked turkey with all the trimmings. The children and I are going there for dinner."

"Oh, I am not invited, is that it?"

"No, that is not it. But you always seem to be going off alone. We do not exclude you from our activities; you exclude yourself. You know that whenever the children and I are invited out the invitation always includes you."

Saturday afternoon, as Chris walked out of the master bedroom he said, "Janice, did I hear you say you were going to the movies?"

"Yes. Wendy and I are going to the movies."

"Which theater are you going to?" he asked.

"I am not sure; we have not decided."

"I have a five o'clock appointment, after which I am going to the office to get a head start on next week's work."

She walked him to his car. Starting the engine he said, "I should be home around nine-thirty."

"Okay, Wendy and I should be back by then."

When Janice walked into the house, Wendy said, "Mom, let's go to the movie on Twenty-sixth Street in Wilton Manors. And Justice for All is playing there and we both like Al Pachino."

"Fine with me, let's go."

They enjoyed the movie, laughing so hard at times they covered their mouths with their hands. It was ludicrous for a grown man to urinate on himself and for a judge to wave a loaded gun in the courtroom. After the movie, Janice said to Wendy, "I am taking you home. If your father is not there, I will drop you off and leave. I will not come home until after he gets home."

Pulling into the driveway, Chris's car was nowhere to be seen. Wendy exited the car and Janice said, "Don't worry. I am going to my parents' home in Pompano for a short visit. I'll see you later."

Janice had not told her daughter the truth; she decided to make sure the rumors she had been hearing were true. She wanted to see for herself. She drove to the shopping center across the street from Chris's office building and parked. A fast-food store was directly across from the office building's parking lot. Janice stood in the restaurant's shadow, watching the front door of the office building. Chris's car was parked under a large tree.

After approximately ten minutes, she saw him come to the door and look toward Oakland Park Boulevard; then he held his left arm to the light and looked at his watch. After standing in the doorway briefly, he went back into the office.

Janice stood in the shadow across the street. He seems to be looking for someone, she thought. Ten minutes later, he was back to the front door looking toward the boulevard. This time, Janice saw a yellow and white Grand Prix turn into the parking lot. A female was alone in the car. He saw the car, walked to the sidewalk, and wait. As the car slowed, he walked to the driver's window, leaned in and talked to the occupant.

Janice moved from the shadows of the building, walking toward the couple. After taking a few faltering steps, she stopped and wondered what to do. She went back into the shadows of the fast-food restaurant. As she turned to look at her husband and the woman, she saw Chris walk to the passenger side and climb inside. Without thinking, Janice again walked toward the parking lot, where the yellow and white Grand Prix was racing toward her, out of the lot.

Janice continued toward the car, which did not waver. The driver was speeding and as the headlights reached her, she heard the woman cry. "There is someone in front of the car!"

The car swerved wildly. As the car passed Janice on the right, she automatically put out her right hand and lifted up. Her hand connected with the door handle and the door on the passenger side opened. She heard her husband yell, "Stop! That's my wife."

The Grand Prix continued down the drive until it reached the street and stopped. Chris jumped out and ran back towards Janice. The Grand Prix left, burning rubber.

Rushing to her he asked, "Honey, what is the matter! Is anything wrong with the children?"

Janice looked with all the piercing pain she felt in her heart showing in her eyes.

"Why, Chris? Just tell me why?"

"Why what?" he laughed. "That is just a client. She stopped by to pay her down payment on a house because she is going out of town for a week."

"If she only stopped to pay her down payment; why did you get into the car with her and where were you going?"

Instead of answering, he asked, "Where did you park your car?" "In the shopping center across the street."

"Go get it and let's go home; I'm hungry."

Chris watched her as she walked toward her car not turning away until she entered the vehicle. He then climbed into his Cutlass and drove off.

Driving home, Janice did not know what to think. She knew what she had seen, but Chris had made her feel stupid. She parked the car under the carport, wondering at the same time if she had driven faster than she realized. Chris was not at home.

An hour later, she heard his key in the lock. The sound of the key in the lock made her feel frightened and nervous.

"Janice," he said, entering the bedroom, "Why did you come to the office?"

"I wanted some bubble gum, and as I came out of the store, I saw our car in the parking lot and decided to keep you company until you had completed working. I thought you might appreciate some company, especially since you have been feeling under the weather lately."

"Chris, who was that woman, why are you doing this to us?"

"Honey, I know it looks bad, but it was not what it seemed. The lady called the house, and the children told her I was at the office. Instead of calling here, she decided to drive here and leave her payment in the mailbox outside."

"If that is the case, why did you get into her car and start to drive off with her?"

"I asked her to go across the street and have a sandwich with me," he replied.

"That is what I am for, you never take me anywhere, yet you ask a client to have a sandwich with you. Every time I ask you to take me somewhere, you don't have any money. I am your wife. I am the one who works and helps you pay the bills, and you want to take another woman out to eat."

Chris said, "Baby, I know it looks bad, but it's not the way it looked. Baby, you have got to trust me. I can't do my job right if you don't trust me."

"Chris, you can't be trusted; you lie and lie, and keep on lying. Our bills are three months or more behind. How can you spend money on someone else when you don't have the money to pay our bills, or when you can't pay for gas to take the children for a ride? That client is not the only woman you spend money on; there are others. Some you take to breakfast, some you take to lunch and some you take to dinner, like this woman tonight."

"Baby, believe me, that is in the past. I won't do it anymore."

"Where is Wendy?" he asked, remembering they had gone to the movies together.

"She has gone to bed. I dropped her off after leaving the movie." Looking hard at his wife, he asked. "Janice, are you all right?"

Without answering she asked, "Chris, why did it take you so long to reach home?"

"I drove around to get some air to clear my head," he replied. He went into the bathroom and came out complaining of dizziness and a headache.

"Do we have any cough medicine?"

"No, we don't," she answered.

"I am going to the pharmacy," he said, walking toward the door. After he left, Janice turned to Beverly and asked, "Beverly did I get any telephone calls tonight?"

"No, Momma, the telephone rang once and it was the wrong number.

Some man asked if this was the animal hospital."

This time, Chris was gone two hours. He looked at Janice as he walked into the bedroom saying, "The pharmacy was closed. Do we have any aspirin?"

"Chris," she said between clenched teeth, "Why did you say that lady had called here and one of the children had told her you were at the office?"

Hearing this, he tensed. His thoughts raced as he tried to remember exactly what he had said. A moment later he replied, "I told you I called her to tell her she was going to lose the house and if she wanted to keep it, she had to pay the down payment. She had just returned from vacation."

Picking up her car keys and walking toward the front door, Janice said. "I need some fresh air this time."

Chris said, "You need what? Go on, do whatever you want to do."

Getting into her Volkswagen, Janice drove without any sense of direction; her mind was on her failing marriage. I will drive to the beach. The calmness of the water should help to steady my nerves.

Consequently, she found herself parking along A-1-A looking out at the dark-blue and lavender water of the Atlantic Ocean. Waves gently washed up on the sandy beach, depositing seaweed, and then gently rolled out again.

After much heartfelt thinking, Janice decided to ignore the entire situation. I am not ready to face this; I will pretend it never happened. Glancing up, she saw a large boat floating slowly in a southerly direction, lights glowing from stem to stern. She watched the boat until it was out of sight, then backed the car from its parking space and headed home.

The next morning, as Janice was clearing the breakfast dishes from the dining-room table, the telephone rang. "Hello," she heard Rodney say as he answered the telephone.

"Momma, telephone call for you," he said.

"This is Janice," she said into the receiver. "What can I do for you?"

The voice replied, "I am going to do something for you; I won't give you my name, but we do know each other. I like you and I am sick and tired of seeing your husband make a complete fool of you. He always tells you he is working late at the office–that's bullshit. He spends his time at a house on Hunter's Lane. Don't take my word for it; anytime he tells you he is going to the office, take a little drive down to Hunter's Lane and see if your car is parked in front of a red and white house."

"Who is this?" she demanded, trying to place the voice. She knew she had heard it before.

After making this statement, the caller quickly hung up, not bothering to answer the question. she thought about the strange telephone call all day, one moment wanting to tell Chris and the next minute wanting to check it out for herself. Maybe I should find out where he spends his time. I know he lies about always being at the office.

Later that night, Chris left for the office. Janice waited an hour, and then headed for Hunter's Lane. Turning off Twenty-Seventh Avenue, the first thing she saw was their car a block and a half down the street. Driving slowly past the red and white house, she noticed a car under the carport. Taking note of the license number, she repeated the number over and over until she turned the corner; there she stopped and wrote the number down. She could not distinguish one car from another, but she did know that each vehicle had its own license-plate number.

Driving home, she had to concentrate on forcing herself not to break down. Crying won't help me now. I need to think; I must think. Reaching home, her mind raced in every direction–round and round, up and down. Not wanting to face what she had seen, she decided to put it from her mind. It could very well be a legitimate visit to a client. I won't say anything. If I ignore it, Chris will soon get tired and stop this foolishness. I will give him time to get it out of his system, if he really is fooling around.

As the week wore on, Chris was gone more than usual. The next time he is gone for a long time, I will go to Hunter's Lane, and if he is there, I will let him know that I know where he spends his time, Janice resolved.

That Saturday afternoon, Chris left for the office as usual, not wearing shorts, but dressed in his regular work clothes. By ten-thirty, he was not home. Janice decided to find out where he was.

The first place she checked was the house on Hunter's Lane. His car was not there, nor was any other vehicle. She decided to drive by the Shore Club. Neither car could be found in that parking lot, but as she continued driving on Second Street, she noticed a familiar car in the parking lot at the Elk's Lodge. The lot was well lighted, but almost empty. Slowing, she drove around the car and noticed the license number. Yes, it was the car from Hunter's Lane. Janice saw a green van parked next to the building. She parked her Volkswagen next to the van where it could not been easily seen. She settled in the seat for a long wait. *I will wait until they show up. I want to see exactly who he is with.*

At one o'clock, lights flashed across the windshield. Holding her head over the dash, Janice saw her husband's car approaching the parking lot. It came to a stop next to the car she had been watching. As it stopped, she noticed two occupants in the car. They talked for five minutes; then the passenger door opened and a woman got out, walked to the driver's door of the yellow and white Grand Prix, which Janice had been watching, and drove away. Janice exited her Volkswagen, and started to walk around the front of the van. The driver of the van started his engine and began to drive away, making her change directions and walk around the rear of the van. As she approached her husband's car, she tapped the window on the passenger side. Chris looked at her as she said, "You can't say I did not catch you this time," pointing her finger at him as she talked. Without giving him a chance to reply, she turned and walked off; noticing at the same time that the Grand Prix had stopped and the woman was looking back. Both vehicles pulled off, one following the other.

Janice drove away with gears clashing. Fifteen minutes later driving past her house, she noticed Chris's car was not there, and she continued past to check the house on Hunter's Lane. On Hunter's Lane, she noticed neither car was there. They must have gone somewhere to talk. I won't go home before he gets there, no matter how late it is.

Janice drove to the other side of town, trying to calm down. As she was heading toward home again, she saw both vehicles driving along Fifteenth Avenue. I'll bet they are going to the house to talk to me. I will not be there.

She turned right, heading for Minnie and Tom's home.

Half an hour later, she finished telling them what had happened by saying she was going to see an attorney first thing the next morning. They both said how sorry they were that things were going bad for her, and offered their help in any way if she needed it.

When Janice finally arrived home, Chris was in the bedroom. She did not say a word. He looked at her as she placed her purse on the chair beside the bed and said, "Janice, what are you trying to do? Why do you keep following me?"

"I did not follow you, you just happened to show up where I was parked. Tell me something Chris. "Why do you take her places and refuse to take me anywhere?"

"I did not take her anywhere. I was with her husband, James earlier and I told him that you thought his wife and I were having an affair. James then invited me to a party and I accepted the invitation."

"Why didn't you call me and invite me to go with you? You knew I was home."

Chris continued looking at her as if he had not heard her. "I did not take her anywhere, as I stated before. I just brought her back to her car."

"If she was with her husband, why did you have to bring her back to her car? Why didn't she ride in the same car with her husband?"

"James was going to work, and she was already at the party when he arrived. He had stopped by the Elk's because he was tired and wanted a drink. That's where we met."

Pulling her night-gown over her head, she replied. "I don't want to hear anymore of your lies. Just shut up."

Chris sat on the edge of the bed and asked if she would like to have sex. "No, definitely not."

"You mean you don't want me?" he asked in a disbelieving voice.

"I don't want a man who does not want me. You try to act as if you want me, but I can tell your body doesn't because your member is always soft in the middle."

Grabbing her gown at the bottom, he pushed it to her chest, climbing on top of her, and tried to enter her, but it was rough going. As he continued trying to force himself onto her, he did not notice how dry she was, which caused her to cry out.

Not realizing he was hurting her and making her sore; Chris said, "I knew you wanted me. You just want to play hard to get. Move! Aren't you going to help me?"

"I do not want you," she said in a dry voice. "Please leave me alone." He continued pushing, his member growing larger and larger.

"Doesn't he realize I am too upset for sex? And even if I was horny before I caught him tonight, catching him would make me forget about sex. If I don't help him, he will not enjoy it.

Before it was over, he looked into her face and said, "I know you are fucking up on me."

She looked at him and said, "You've got to be crazy. I have never gone anywhere without the children until lately and you know it." For the past three weeks, Janice had started going out every night to try to make him jealous, hoping it would make him stay at home or take her with him.

He finally stiffened, grunted, rolled over, and fell asleep.

Chapter Twenty-One

On New Year's Day, Chris came out of the bedroom. "I am going to get a pack of cigarettes, and then going to the office. I have about an hour's work I need to get out."

"Good, I'll go with you."

"Why?" he quickly asked.

"Because I want to be with you and I have nothing else to do. I am reading Chesapeake, and I can do that at the office while you are working."

She noticed how hard he was staring at her. She also knew that when the muscles worked like that he was lying. Now, the muscles in his left jaw were working overtime. She knew whenever the muscles worked in his jaw like that, he was thinking very fast and very hard. She also knew he did not want her to go with him because he was not going to the office as he had stated.

Before he could think of some reason for her not to accompany him, Rodney and Beverly, who had been watching television said "Yes, Daddy, let her go with you."

As he hesitated, Janice said, "I'll be ready to go as soon as I get my shoes and purse."

Chris drove straight to the office. Janice noticed he did not stop for cigarettes, but she said nothing. In less than an hour, they were on their way back home.

When they neared a Seven-Eleven, she said, "Don't forget to stop for cigarettes."

Chris continued driving, pulling at his hair, his left arm propped on the window of the car. He seemed to be lost in thought and drove past the store. Reaching home, she went into the den where the children were, and Chris went into the bedroom. Five minutes later, he walked out of the bedroom, into the living room, glanced toward the den and said, "Janice, I'm going to Ivory's for a package of cigarettes. I won't be long."

Four hours later, he had still not returned. Janice said to the children, "Your father must have had to grow the tobacco for his cigarettes. I am going to find him."

She had no idea where to look. She no longer knew his hangouts. It had been a long time since they had gone anywhere together. All their friends seemed to have changed–not really changed; they just did not see them anymore. Then she remembered Hunter's Lane; no luck there. The second place she tried was Troy's, on the corner of Wingate Road (Thirty-first Avenue) and Sunrise Boulevard. Driving through the parking lot at a slow pace, looking for her husband's car, and feeling embarrassed and angry at the same time, her mind would not leave her along.

Do I really want to find him? Do I want to see again that the rumors are true? I already know the communication lines between us have been cut and severed completely. When I try to talk to him he says, 'I don't want to hear your damn nagging.' Even if I try to tell him about the children getting out of hand, he calls it nagging. I can't talk to him unless he starts the conversation. If I start talking first he calls it nagging.

With her thoughts running rampant in her head, Janice pulled onto Sunrise Boulevard again and headed across town to the Elks Lodge. She did not see his car and continued east on Second Street until she came to the Shore Club. Turning south on Fifth Avenue, she did not see anything that resembled her husband's car. Turning her Volkswagen, she saw what she was looking for on the east side of the avenue. Parked in the middle of a vacant lot on the corner was Chris's car. Her heart started pounding in her chest. *Oh, my God, I can't fool myself any longer. I have been blocking this out, telling myself the rumors were just that . . . rumors.*

Parking next to her husband's car, she walked to the Shore club, but she did not enter; she did not know what to expect. Pausing in front of the entrance and glancing through the glass, she did not see Chris.

Walking along the side of the building, she tried to look in the windows, but all the shades seemed to be pulled down. She noticed light streaming from a small opening at the bottom of the last window toward the front of the building. Rushing to the window, she bumped into a man trying to enter the club.

"Sorry," she said without looking up, continuing toward the window.

Peering through the small opening, she saw a row of tables along the inside wall. Some tables were empty and some were occupied. Looking slowly and trying to take a slow, deep breath, she forced herself to look at each occupant, not wanting to mistake someone for Chris; he was not on this side. Retracing her steps, she advanced to the other side of the club. There was a door on this side with a diamond-shaped window in the top center half. Being of short stature, she had to stand on tip toes to see inside. At first, she did not see anything; standing on the sidewalk trying to get a glimpse of the inside of the dark club was nearly impossible.

Not realizing what the problem was, Janice stood back and looked hard. Over the diamond-shaped glass was a piece of aluminum foil. She could not see inside because of the foil.

She instantly balled her fist and hit the door as hard as she could. After hitting it twice, the door suddenly swung open. Bringing down her fist, she did not at first see the man standing I front of her. Realizing her fist had hit something softer; Janice opened her eyes and found herself staring at a complete stranger.

"The front door is always open. You don't have to knock this one down to get in," he stated.

Glancing past him, she looked at the patrons of the club. Chris was not there. Without replying, she turned and walked away.

'What do I do next?' she wondered. Two buildings from the club was a church. Walking toward it, she decided to wait. She knew he had to return to his car, and she wanted to be there when he did.

It was very cold on this New Year's night, and the wind was blowing in the direction she was standing. Next to the church, directly on the corner, was an apartment building. In front of this building was a large truck with wooden slats on the sides. Walking to the back of this truck to see if she could hide behind it, Janice realized the truck as filled with construction equipment.

Peering around, she saw a set of wrought-iron lawn furniture next to the truck. Pulling one of the chairs behind her, she placed it as close to the truck as possible. Putting it into position where the truck would block the cold wind and where she could see the front of the club as well as her husband's car. Sitting, she said, "What the hell am I doing? The Hawk is freezing my ass off and I'm trying to see something I know will break my heart. "I am going home," she said aloud, as she raised herself from the lawn chair.

Standing where she was in the dark, she glanced towards the door of the Shore Club again. Seeing a car moving towards her, her heart began to beat so loud in her chest that she knew if someone was near they would be able to hear every beat. The car was not the car she was waiting to see. She was looking for a white over yellow Grand Prix, and this one was dark in color.

Getting into her Volkswagen and driving off, Janice was not sure if she wanted to know for sure this time or not. I will destroy everything by my actions tonight. I am going home.

Janice was a block away from home when an inner voice said, don't be a fool. You know enough now to know which way your life with Chris is going. You will either have to accept it or put a stop to it. Either way, it can no longer be ignored.

Making a U-turn at Turner's Corner, Janice headed back across town. Deciding not to park where Chris could see her car when he returned, she parked in the parking lot of Benton's Funeral Home, close to a hearse.

It seemed to have grown colder during the minutes she had been gone. As she neared the truck, instead of sitting in the lawn chair, she dropped to her knees and crawled beneath the truck. She found it to be much warmer. Peering from under the truck, she could see her husband's car. Crawling on all fours to the other side of the truck, she could not see the door of the club. Continuing to crawl to the end of the truck, she found that she could see the complete front of the club. Smiling, she knew she could wait until she froze or until hell froze over, whichever came first.

Twenty minutes later, Janice saw the car she had been waiting for drive up and stop directly in front of the truck she was lying under. It was too dark to see the occupants clearly, but she heard a cough and recognized her husband's voice as he muttered something.

Just as I thought; he is with the same bitch. I am going to confront them both. Crawling from under the truck, her mind racing, what am I supposed to say? This made her stop. Sitting again, fool, stop procrastinating. You will have to fish or cut bait; the choice is yours.

At this time Janice heard the motor of the car start. Quickly, she moved back beneath the truck. The driver of the yellow car drove forward approximately two car lengths and parked on the shoulder of the roadway. The occupants seemed to settle down for a long talk.

Given a respite, Janice tried to calm down. This has to be followed through. I can no longer allow myself to continue going through the ups and down of a three-sided relationship. I will wait and confront him alone. No use making a fool of myself in front of her. If he did not want to see her, he would not be with her. She cannot make him do anything he doesn't want to do.

Just as she was about to give up, she heard the door of the car open. Lifting her head from her chest, she saw Chris step from the passenger side of the automobile and walk toward her car. The car he had exited pulled away immediately at a slow pace, its lights off. Halfway to his car he saw her walking toward him. Startled, he said, "Honey, what are you doing here?"

Looking into his eyes, "What do you have to say now?" she asked him. "Nothing," he answered. "I can't say a thing. Baby, why are you doing this to me? It's just a coincidence that she came up as I came out of the Shore Club. I just sat over there and talked with her for ten or fifteen minutes, that's all."

"No, Chris, you are lying again; you drove up with her. Then she pulled onto the shoulder of the road and the two of you sat there for almost an hour. I have been here since nine-thirty, sitting where I could see the door of the club and your car."

"Baby, I was with Jerome Markham. I stopped by his mother's house and he asked me to go to the airport with him. We took his sister to Fort Lauderdale International Airport. She is on vacation and–"

"Stop!" she yelled. "Just stop your lying. What is her name Chris?"

"Baby, I am not lying. Her name is Pat DeWitt. I know it looks funny, but as I was coming out of the lounge, she was passing by. She asked me who the lady was Saturday night, and when I answered, my wife, she said, 'oh, shit, you men.'"

As Chris continued lying, Janie knew her love for him had died. She also remembered the telephone call years ago when the lady called about the car insurance. She remained dry-eyed as she continued looking into his face. She felt calm inside; the inner turmoil she had been feeling melted away. She felt as if a large weight had been lifted from her shoulders. She wondered, what kind of a fool does he take me to be? I may not believe all the rumors I hear, but I sure as hell believe my own eyes. "Come on baby, let's go home."

"You go ahead, I don't know if I'll come straight home or not," she answered.

"Where did you park your car?" he asked with a frown. "Don't worry about that," she replied and walked away.

He drove slowly down the street until he saw her reach her car. That was the last place he would have looked, for he knew she was afraid of the dead. After seeing the car, he knew she was alone and did not have a witness. He drove away; she did not go directly home.

Chapter Twenty-Two

Sunday evening, as Janice drove into Louise's driveway to pick her up for a class meeting, her friend called out, "Park your car along the easement; it's my turn to drive."

The class meeting ended early because they did not have a quorum. Instead of leaving, the adjourned meeting turned into a gossip session.

Later in the evening, as she drove away from Louise's home, Janice wondered if Chris was home. Pulling into the drive a few minutes later, she noticed her husband's car was not there. She did not drive completely into the carport, but stopped in the driveway and blew her horn. When the children came to the door, she asked where their father was. Rodney answered, "He left twenty minutes after you did this evening. He said he was going to get a pack of cigarettes and would be right back."

"Thanks, Rod," I know where he is. I'll be back in about ten minutes."

Janice backed out of the driveway burning rubber. Not only was she burning rubber, she was burning with rage as she headed for the house on Hunter's Lane. She slowed the Volkswagen as she neared the house she was looking for. There, parked directly in front of the bungalow, was Chris's car. Janice looked to make sure it was her husband's car. She did not stop but kept driving, heading straight for home. She pulled into the driveway on two wheels. As she exited the vehicle, she turned back inside the car and pressed the handle that made the front seat lean forward. Leaving the car door open, she entered the house, going directly to the master bedroom. Walking to the chest of drawers, she pulled open the top drawer which held Chris's socks and underwear. Grabbing an armload, she ran outside and dumped the garments on the back seat of the car. Running back inside, she collided with the children.

"Momma, what's wrong with you?" they asked. "What are you doing?" "Go to bed," she said over her shoulder as she re-entered the bedroom.

"This does not concern you."

The children looked at each other, unsure of what to do. This time Janice came from the bedroom with her arms loaded with shirts and slacks. She could hardly see where she was walking, the load was so large.

"Didn't I tell you to go to bed?" she yelled. "You have school tomorrow and you know how you hate to get up in the mornings." They slowly turned and went into their bedrooms.

Janice threw the clothing into the back of the little car and pulled the seat back in place. At the front door, she turned the lock on the knob and shut the door, trying the handle to make sure the door was locked. She drove back to Hunter's Lane, sedately this time.

In a few minutes, Janice was back in front of the house on the lane. She did not drive onto the property, but stopped her car in the street, next to her husband's car. As she got out of her car, she saw the curtain at the kitchen window move. She left the motor of her car running as she leaned into the back of the VW and removed an armful of clothing.

Walking around her car, she placed the clothing on the hood of Chris's car and pushed them as hard as she could. At this point, the front door of the bungalow opened and Chris and Pat DeWitt came out of the house.

Chris said, "Janice, what do you think you are doing?"

"I am doing something you don't have the nerve to do," she replied. "This is where you want to be, and this is where I want you to be. I don't want any man that doesn't want me."

Janice looked at Pat and said, "You can have him. He won't stay away from you so he may as well move in with you." Janice turned and headed for her car.

In a loud voice, Chris said, "Janice, take my clothes back home."

"No, Chris. I've asked you to stay away from Pat, and you won't. Now I am asking you to stay away from me."

Janice entered her VW and looked up. Chris was walking around the back of her Volkswagen. She immediately locked the door and rolled up the window. She waited for him to grab the handle and open the door. When he grabbed the door handle, Janice put the Volkswagen into gear and pulled off as fast as she could, pulling his arm until he released the handle. She heard him yell over the loud noise of the little car, "I'll be right home."

By the time Chris arrived home with his clothes, Janice had showered and was in bed.

Chris awoke Janice from a sound sleep wanting to make love. "Leave me alone. I want to sleep," she mumbled.

He refused to leave her alone and continued trying to rouse her.

Not long afterwards, Janice came wide awake, saying, "Stop shaking me! Can't you see I'm trying to sleep?"

"Look at the sheet, he insisted, I'm pitching a tent."

She looked him directly in the eyes and said, "Why not take the tent and what's under it to your whore? She is the one you want. I just happen to be the one you are stuck with."

A few minutes later, the alarm sounded. Presently, as Janice came out of the bathroom, Chris said, "Honey, do me a favor and wear your sexy underwear to work today."

Not wanting another argument, Janice complied. As Chris watched her put on the panties with no crotch, and the bra with holes that her nipples poked through, the tent he was pitching rose higher.

At this point, Chris rushed from the bed, grabbed her and started kissing her earlobes and the side of her neck. He knew that this always turned her on.

Bringing his right hand to her left nipple, he rubbed her breast in small circles, whispering, "You make something on me harder than Superman's kneecap."

Instead of being turned on, Janice became furious. Pushing with all her might, she screamed, "Take your filthy hands off me! I don't love you and I don't want you touching me. After the way you've treated me, how can you possibly think I want your lips and hands on my body? I'll do without forever before I allow myself to be used by you. I bought this underwear a year ago to bring excitement into our lovemaking, and you were not interested. Now, all of a sudden you want me to wear it."

As she talked, Chris lay across the bed and listened. Janice pulled on a dark-blue skirt and matching long-sleeved blouse with a cowl neck from the closet. After dressing, she fumbled through the jewelry box and pulled out a long silver necklace, a pair of silver earrings, and a silver bracelet.

"Furthermore," she continued, "not only do I not want you to touch me, I don't want you in this house. Why don't you move to Hunter's Lane?"

As she delivered this speech, she slammed out of the house yelling. "I've got to get out of this damn house before he drives me crazy."

"Chris I will not live like this anymore," Janice said to him later that night. "You won't live like what?" he asked.

"The past two years have been hell. No human being should be subjected to the type of mental abuse you have put me through," she replied in a sad voice. "I'll let you know what I am going to do when I reach a decision, but I definitely will not continue to live as we are living now."

"Stop following me everywhere I go," he said.

Chris had decided that Janice was just letting off steam. She won't like being without a man. She is not going to do anything. All she needs is a long session of good lovemaking and she'll be content to let me come and go as I please.

Chris came out of the bedroom, through the living room, and into the kitchen, saying, to Janice, "I am going to the station for gas."

Wendy said, "Take me with you dad. I need to stop at Burger King to pick up my paycheck."

"Okay," he replied, which surprised Wendy. He never wanted to take them anywhere. His normal reply was, 'ask your mother to take you.'

Twenty minutes later they were back. "Did you get your gas," Janice asked.

"No, all the stations except the one on the corner of Twenty-seventh and Sunrise had long lines. I'll fill up later."

Janice looked at him and wondered why he could not fill up the tank with Wendy in the car. Why go later? Twenty minutes later he left to get his gas. Janice waited five minutes, then left to follow him. Chris drove directly to the house on Hunter's Lane.

Janice pulled to a stop in front of the little house where Chris had parked and blew her horn. A curtain at the front window moved, but no one came to the door. Deciding not to wait to see if he came out, Janice turned the ignition off; pulled on the parking brake, and reached for the door handle of the little Volkswagen. Just as she pulled the door of the car open, the front door of the house opened and Chris walked toward her. As he walked around the rear end of his vehicle, Janice said, "I want you to get your clothes from home and move them here. This is where you spend all your time."

Chris kept walking toward the Volkswagen, but Janice pulled off before he could say anything.

Racing up Thirty-First Avenue, the traffic signal at Thirty-first and Sunrise changed, forcing her to hit hard on the brakes. She was about the third vehicle back. Looking in her rear-view mirror, she saw Chris driving in the lane next to her. He stopped his car next to her Volkswagen and started talking to her. She rolled down the window on the passenger side of the little car, and he started laughing, saying, "I got gas in my car."

She replied, "You probably had gas all the time–that was just your excuse to leave the house. I am tired of you lying, and I want you out of the house."

"I did not see the lady who lives there. I was talking to her husband."

"I don't care who you were talking with–her husband, her son, her brother, her roommate, or any of her relatives–I don't give a shit. That's where you are all the time, and that is where I want you to be."

Janice did not notice she was yelling at the top of her lungs and that the people in the vehicles around them were staring. The traffic signal turned green. Chris merged his car in front of Janice's Volkswagen. With gears clashing, she tried to cut him off and not let him in, but he was too fast. There were three vehicles separating them. Chris was driving like a bat out of hell. As Janice pulled up and stopped at the traffic signal at Thirty-First and Nineteenth Street, she did not see his car. She made her right turn onto Nineteenth Street as the signal turned green. Driving east on Nineteenth, she saw his car coming toward Nineteenth on Thirtieth Way. He had driven back to make sure she was coming home, and not going elsewhere. They pulled up to the house at the same time.

As they walked into the house, Janice said, "I want you out–and I mean out!"

Chris kept telling her there was nothing going on and he was tired of her following him. They sat on the sofa in the living room, and as they continued arguing, Janice lifted her right hand to point at him, but her arm froze at an angle in mid-air. She could not move her hand; she looked closely at her hand: her thumb was folded under and all five fingers were stiff, her hand and arm had broken out into small wrinkles, and the entire arm was trembling.

She cried, "Oh my God, I am having a stroke."

Chris said, "Baby, you are doing this to yourself. Why don't you lie down?

You need to lie down. Your nerves are the cause of this."

She told him not to touch her. He was the cause of her problems and her problems would be solved as soon as he left.

"I am losing my mind," she said as she walked away from Chris into the master bathroom and swallowed two aspirin and climbed into bed. Taking deep breaths, she forced herself to count slowly and think of something pleasant. Half an hour later, she could feel herself relaxing; the tension had slowly begun to leave her body, and her arm was beginning to feel normal again.

Chapter Twenty-Three

One morning in early February, Janice forgot to take her heater to work, and returned home to get it. The office she worked in was air-conditioned, but it had no heat. As she pulled into her driveway, she saw Florida Power & Light trucks in front of the house making a loud racket; they were wiring the new light poles that had been installed. Janice exited the car, and as she neared the front of the house she heard. "I hear someone coming; wait a minute."

Janice saw Chris's face appear at the window, and then disappear. "I have to hang up now; my wife is home."

Janice walked into Rodney's bedroom, picked up the heater, turned and left without uttering one sound. As she exited the door, Chris asked if anything was wrong. She slammed the door and kept walking. When she was back at the office, she called and told him he should not have hung-up because she had come home. "You could have continued talking to your bitch."

He yelled into the receiver, "You are crazy! Do you know that? Crazy! You don't even know what you are talking about."

"I am not crazy," she replied in a calm voice. "I know what I heard and I don't consider myself your wife anymore."

After a minute of silence, he hung up.

The next day, Wendy came home early from her classes at Broward Community College. As she approached the door, she heard her father dial the telephone and then ask, "How is everything?" After a slight pause, he said, "I'll see what I can do. I will have to cash a check."

When Janice returned home, Wendy told her what she heard her father say on the telephone. Janice did some thinking and told Wendy and Beverly that she was going to tell Chris she wanted a divorce.

He called at six-thirty that evening to ask Janice what she had cooked for supper.

"I baked a chicken, and I want you to know that I have made up my mind as to what I am going to do."

"Do, about what?" he asked.

"I told you that I had to make up my mind about what I was going to do when I caught you with your girlfriend. Remember, you asked me what I was going to do?"

"Oh, well, I am at a client's home now. I think I'll come home before going to the office."

Janice left twenty minutes later and went to Louise's home. Ever since she had caught Chris with his girlfriend, she had been going out every night. Sometimes she went to the main branch of the library on Sunrise Boulevard next to Holiday Park; other times she visited different friends and relatives. Tonight she wanted to remain home and watch Damien on television, but since she had stayed home last night, she felt she must go out. She returned at 11:15 and went directly to bed.

Chris came home fifteen minutes later and asked what she had been talking about on the telephone about making up her mind. She told him she wanted a legal separation. He looked at her and said, "You must be crazy. I get tired of this foolishness."

Shaking inside, but knowing she had to say what was on her mind, she replied. "You don't seem to be able to stay away from her. Why don't you just move out and live with her?"

Chris went into the den, and turned on the television. After five minutes, he turned the television off, walked back into the bedroom saying, "I'll tell you what, Janice, why don't you get out? You are the one who is not satisfied, so why don't you just leave?"

"There is nothing wrong with you except the fact that your conscience is bothering you," she yelled at him.

"I'll get you for this," he yelled back. "Just say something about this tomorrow, and I will show you. I will get you, so help me."

"Do that Chris, and be sure to own up to the fact that you sent me straight to my attorney's office."

The next morning as she was dressing for work, the telephone rang. The same nameless voice that called her every so often asked if Chris was supposed to be at the office last night.

"Yes, as a matter of fact he was."

The voice laughed at this and Janice asked, "Why do you ask? Did you see him?"

"Yes, I saw him, but not at the office. He was on Hunter's Lane again. It was around nine-thirty, and he was saying that when he first came home from the Army, you had saved a large sum of money. He bragged about sitting in Little Joe's bar every day while you thought he was job hunting on the beach."

Remembering the one-hundred-dollar bank account, she said, "I think you for your help. You have helped me make up my mind."

Without saying a word to Chris, she finished dressing and went to work.

Chapter Twenty-Four

Janice was forced to realize her marriage was not going to get better. She also knew she had to do some very serious thinking. To do this, she felt the best place to go to be completely alone–yet not along–was Holiday Park. Thus, as she drove her Volkswagen east along Sunrise Boulevard, she did not notice any of the passing scenery. As a consequence, she was startled by the honking of a horn and was surprised to see that she was straddling the white line that divided the lanes of traffic. Jerking the steering wheel to the right, she glanced around to take note of her surroundings. She was in front of King Oldsmobile, and knew the entrance to the park was a block away.

She turned on the right signal, slowing to make her turn into the park. As she made her turn, she noticed a large fighter airplane, painted in sparkling white with blue writing on its side, anchored down at the entrance to Holiday Park. Continuing for approximately two hundred yards, she made another right turn. To her dismay, she saw that the parking lot to her left was full. To her right, a lively game of football was being played on the field across from the parking lot. Behind the parking lot on her left was a large, lifelike train for children to play. Just beyond the train was a basketball court on which a noisy game was in progress. Janice continued driving past War Memorial Auditorium, which was surrounded by plush green grass–a golfer's delight. Located on this side of the park was the tennis court, a doubles' match in progress, and the gymnasium. She pulled into the parking lot in front of the gymnasium.

Sitting in her car and looking across the park, she did not see the many trees around her, nor did she take note of the joggers running past–young and old, male and female.

Leaving the car, she walked in a southerly direction. She was jarred into the present by a loud game in progress on the paddleball court, which was on the outside wall of the gymnasium. Watching the game allowed her to forget her inner turmoil for a few seconds. However, as she stood there, everything came rushing into memory. Starting to walk again, she began to notice her surroundings and the activity around her. Walking past the shuffleboard court, the path made a U-turn behind War Memorial Auditorium. Deciding not to continue along the jogging course, she turned and started walking, with bended head, across the plush green grass. Bending down to pick up a fallen pine-cone, she suddenly felt dizzy.

"I can't deal with this," she said aloud, as if she was talking to someone. Sitting at one of the many picnic tables, she began to think how dramatically the life of her family had changed. She and the children were accustomed to going on different outings. From the beginning, they were never a stay-at- home family, always going to the movies, to the beach, on pleasant drives down to the Keys, or to Disney World.

Am I willing to continue living like this? The answer is no. what can I do about it? Do I want a divorce, or would I really prefer a legal separation?

Janice decided she wanted a divorce after thinking things out thoroughly. She did not want to remain attached to Chris in any way, form, or fashion. She was proud of her children; they were among the few worthwhile accomplishments remaining from her shattered marriage.

I have money in a safe deposit box where I keep the savings bonds I receive through payroll deduction, she mused. The Lord will make a way for me to survive. Undoubtedly, things have gotten worse. The time has come for me to fend for myself.

After about two hours, Janice had made up her mind. She would ask him to visit a marriage counselor with her. If he refused, she would visit the counselor alone.

Later the next morning, she broached the subject. "Chris, I would like for us to visit a marriage counselor."

"Why?" he asked. "We don't have any reason to see anyone like that."

"We do, Chris. Please, let me make an appointment for us."

"You can make anything you want to make for yourself," he replied. "I don't have any problems. If you want to see a shrink, go ahead, but don't involve me."

"Chris, we do have a problem, a serious problem. We no longer talk to each other. Every time you come home at night and I speak to you, I get yelled at. Something is very wrong between us, and since you refuse to talk about it, maybe you will be able to talk to a counselor."

"If there is a problem here, I don't have it; maybe you should see someone," he stated. "As a matter of fact, I wish you would see someone. You are driving me crazy with your insecurity."

Janice called Henderson Clinic on Monday morning and was given an appointment.

Walking into the counselor's office ten o'clock the next day, she introduced herself to the first person she saw. "I'm Janice Blunt." Smiling she shook he older woman's hand.

"I have a ten o'clock appointment with Dr. McLemore."

"I am Dr. McLemore," the woman replied. "Please sit and make yourself comfortable."

After filling out the necessary forms, Dr. McLemore asked Janice to tell her why she thought she needed counseling. Starting out very slowly, Janice began talking. When she had finished talking, Dr. McLemore asked if she felt that she had tried everything in her power to work things out with her husband.

"Yes, I have bent over sideways and every other way a person can bend, but nothing seemed to make him want to try to work at our marriage."

"Mrs. Blunt, you are here for my professional advice and I will give it to you. I advise you to get out of that marriage as fast as you can. You said yourself that in the beginning you stayed in this marriage for your children's sake. You later found out that your children knew more of what was going on than you did. You also have said that your son is giving you all sorts of trouble.

"You may not realize it, but staying in this marriage is part of what is making your son act the way he is acting. There is no hope in this marriage as long as your husband refuses to recognize the fact that what he is doing is wrong. Get a divorce before you start having more serious problems with your son. After you and the children are separated from Mr. Blunt, you will soon begin to notice the improvement in your son's behavior. My recommendation to you is two-fold: let me give you a prescription for a tranquilizer and file for divorce as soon as possible."

"I was hoping for another solution. I never believed in divorce, but I cannot continue living as I have these past years. All right, Dr. McLemore, I will not let anything or anyone cause me to start popping pills, but I will file for divorce as soon as I can get the money."

Driving back to work after her appointment, Janice could barely see through her tears. *I hoped it would never come to this point. I am surprised that since this was my first visit, the counselor recommended divorce so quickly. How will I tell my parents? How will I tell our friends?*

Crying harder, she thought, *Oh, my God, please help me. I am putting everything in your hands, God. I can't deal with this right now; I must have time to adjust to the big change I am going to put my family through, I will pick it up later, after I have adjusted a little. I won't leave it with you for long, because you have enough problems, and I must do my part before I give it over to you permanently.*

Driving back to work became too much for Janice. She was forced to pull to the side of Broward Boulevard until she could get her feelings under control. Placing her head on the steering wheel of the little car, she pounded the dashboard and let the flow of tears come. Fifteen minutes later, she dried her face and continued traveling east along Broward until she reached the Interstate. *I will never go through anything this painful again. For a man who is supposed to love me, Chris has given an Academy Award-winning performance of just the opposite. I wonder if there was anything specific I did to make him stop loving me?*

Pulling into the parking lot of the office building Janice made a firm decision to stop the flow of tears. She did not want her co-workers to know of her private turmoil.

Should I ask someone about an attorney? I know nothing about this sort of thing. I want an attorney who will look out for my interest. Dear Lord, please guide me.

All these things raced through Janice's mind. She had decided to give one more try to saving her marriage by visiting a marriage counselor, and the counselor had very firmly told her to end her marriage. "You are not helping your children by remaining in this situation," the female counselor had said.

Janice could hardly concentrate on her work for the remainder of the day. That evening, after helping the children with their schoolwork, she sat to read the Fort Lauderdale News, which was her usual routine. After reading Ann Landers, she turned to the next page, and caught her breath; there, before her eyes, was an advertisement in large bold print: "DIVORCES FOR $75." *She could not believe her eyes. This advertisement was placed here for me to see.*

Fate *is not giving me time to talk myself out of a divorce*, she thought, walking to her sewing machine for a pair of scissors to cut the advertisement from the page.

Without saying a word to the children, or anyone, she called the number listed and made an appointment with the attorney.

Janice's appointment with Attorney Cline was at four-thirty in the afternoon. As she parked in the parking lot of the Broward County Courthouse, she was trembling so badly she could not pull the key out of the ignition switch. Taking a deep breath, holding it, and counting to ten helped steady her hands, and the key slipped from the lock with ease.

She walked from the parking lot through the back doors of the courthouse and through the lobby. She was too upset to notice the admiring glances she received from the gentlemen standing around in groups. Passing through the front doors, she was forced to wait for traffic to slow before crossing the street. Attorney Cline's office was on the fifth floor of the tall white building in front of the courthouse.

After meeting Attorney Cline, she was at a loss as to how to tell him what she wanted. Finally, after waiting for her to speak, Attorney Cline asked if she would like a glass of water.

"No, thank you," she replied. "I would like to file for a divorce from my husband. I can pay you one hundred fifty dollars on your fee."

"All right, Mrs. Blunt, just answer a few questions for me."

He wrote the answers she gave him on a long, yellow legal pad. Finished with his questions, he said. "The cost of the divorce is five hundred dollars, if your husband does no fight it. If he does fight the divorce, the cost could be as much as seven hundred dollars."

"The newspaper ad said seventy-five dollars. How did you reach a figure of five hundred to seven hundred dollars?" she asked.

"That is just the first consultation fee. If you decide to give our firm your business, the seventy-five dollars will be deducted from the five-hundred dollar figure."

"I cannot afford to pay for this divorce. I would like to request my husband pay in the petition."

Digging into her purse, Janice pulled out the cash. "I had some savings bonds with my husband as co-owner. I've cashed them in to use the money as my down payment. The remainder of your fee will have to come from Mr. Blunt," she stated as she gave the lawyer her money.

"I'll have my secretary write a receipt. Wait here until I return."

Returning, Attorney Cline continued, "I will put it in the petition that you request attorney fees. You have three children and have invested nineteen years of your life into this marriage, but you can only get child support for one child because he is the only minor; the other two are considered adults. You are also eligible for rehabilitation for two years."

"What is rehabilitation?"

"That is alimony. You can also request the use of his half of the house until your son reaches the age of eighteen; then the court will have the house appraised and it will be put up for sale. Whatever the sale brings, all outstanding debts will be paid, and the remaining balance will then be divided between you and your ex-husband."

"I would rather buy him out in two years, if that is an option."

"The court will decide what is to be done. I will have my secretary draw up the necessary papers; they should be ready to be filed at the courthouse in two weeks. Take this form along with you and bring it back, filled in, next Tuesday. It is a financial report."

"Thank you, Attorney Cline. I will drop this off next week and make an appointment with your secretary for the same time two weeks from today."

What have I done? She wondered as she drove home through the heavy downtown traffic.

Two weeks later, Janice found herself across the desk from Attorney Cline, reading the papers they would file at the courthouse within the hour. She was asking for custody of Rodney, twenty-five dollars per week child support, the use of his half of the house for two years, rehabilitation for two years, and attorney fees. She felt as if she was the one doing wrong. It kept going through her mind that if only she had tried a little harder, things might not have gotten so bad. Instead of asking Chris to talk to her about whatever was wrong, she should have insisted he talk to her.

As they entered the courthouse, Attorney Cline led her past the elevators to the stairway. There was construction in progress on the second floor and the elevators did not stop there.

Reaching the second floor, Janice was out of breath and breathing hard. Even though she had lost twenty-six pounds in the last twenty-six days the front of her thighs felt as if they were on fire. Attorney Cline was on the fat side, but he was breathing easy.

All the clerks were busy. As Janice and Attorney Cline stood waiting, she asked him about a peace warrant. He told her that a restraining order was only necessary if there seemed to be a possibility of violence. Since her husband had never been a violent person, he doubted the judge would issue one.

After they had filed the divorce papers, they went looking for a judge who had a few minutes to spare. They could not find a judge with free time. One secretary made an appointment for them to see a judge on Friday evening.

Janice told Attorney Cline that she was afraid of what would happen when Chris received his divorce papers. "It is true that he has never been a violent person but I am taking away something he considers his. I am really scared that he may become violent and wish you would try to get a judge to grant a restraining order."

"I will call a judge who I think may be sympathetic and try to obtain a restraining order," Attorney Cline said.

Three days later, Attorney Cline notified her that he had found a sympathetic judge who would grant the restraining order.

The following Friday, they found the judge in his chambers, and he issued the restraining order. It cost Janice one dollar to file it with the court.

Two weeks later, on a Monday, Wendy called Janice at work. "Momma," she said in a frightened voice, "I think Daddy's papers are here. I have just had to sign for papers a man from the courthouse left."

"Where is your father?"

"He's not here. He called and said he would be home later."

"Are the papers sealed in and envelope?" "No, they are just folded twice."

"Open it and tell me what they are," Janice instructed her daughter.

Janice heard the rustle of paper as Wendy opened he document. "It has restraining order at the top of it," she said into the telephone.

Janice experienced a let-down feeling. Why, she thought to herself, did the restraining order come before the divorce papers? The divorce papers were filed four days before she had been granted the restraining order.

An hour later, Wendy called again to tell Janice that Chris had been home. He had came home, been given the papers, had looked at them and left the house again. Before he left, Wendy heard him on the telephone in the bedroom telling someone he had received some papers but he did not know what it meant.

Janice was afraid to go home after work. When she arrived, Chris had not returned.

Thirty minutes after Janice arrived from work, she heard a car in the drive. Wendy glanced through the picture window and said, "Momma, Daddy's home."

A wave of terror rushed through her from the top of her head to the bottom of her feet. Should I run out the back door, should I hide in one of the other bedrooms, or should I stand here and face him in front of the children? He won't get out of hand in front of them. Deciding to remain where she was, she took a deep breath and then slowly exhaled.

Chris walked in as if nothing out of the ordinary had happened. "Are you going to cook?" he asked. He looked into the kitchen noticing there were no pots on the stove.

"No, I'm not," she replied. "The children and I are going to Burger King." She kept waiting for him to explode, or ask her what was the purpose of the restraining order, but he did not.

The next few days were like walking on pins and needles. Janice thought Chris would ask at any given time about the papers, but he did not mention a thing.

The following Friday morning, Wendy again called her mother at work.

"Momma, the same man was here and left another legal looking document for Daddy. I had to sign for this one too."

"Open it and read it to me," Janice asked her daughter.

"It is the divorce papers Momma. I don't want to be here when Daddy gets home and see these papers."

"Don't be afraid dear, when he sees the papers, he won't want you to know what they are. He will do his best to act normal in front of you. When he comes home, I want you to act as you usually act–watch cartoons in your bedroom. That way, you won't have to worry about him looking at you and realizing you know what the papers mean."

"Yes, Momma, I'll be in my room where he can't see me," Wendy said, her voice trembling.

"And Wendy, please don't say anything to Beverly or Rodney. I want them kept in the dark about this for now. I will explain it to them later."

"Okay Momma."

After the conversation with her daughter, Janice was too upset to concentrate. Getting up from her desk, she began walking around the office. *What have I done? We have nineteen years invested in each other, and I am destroying all of it. I can't blame myself for the failure of our marriage; it takes two to make a marriage, but it only takes one cold-hearted, unfeeling partner to destroy a marriage. I've tried and tried to make our marriage work, but Chris would not work with me. I've always made it perfectly clear that I do not believe in divorce. He has been banking on that fact to do whatever he wanted to do, and now I have totally surprised him by filing for divorce.*

Sitting at her desk again, she tried to proof read a report. Fifteen minutes later, she was still on the first page of the report. *I cannot concentrate on a damn thing other than my personal troubles. My employer is not getting his money's worth out of me today.* Throughout the remainder of the day, Bessie, her supervisor and friend, kept asking if she was all right.

"You seem to be staring into space or daydreaming a lot lately. Is there anything I can do?"

"Please come in and close the door. I need to unburden myself on someone. I don't expect you to make any comments, just to listen."

She talked and cried for an hour. Bessie listened and cried with her. As Janice finished talking, Bessie suggested she take the remainder of the day off and go home.

"I can't go home now; Chris will be there until four o'clock. I will remain here until my usual quitting time; he should be gone by then. I don't know what I'll do if he causes any trouble."

At four o'clock, she called home to make sure Chris had left at his usual time.

"No, Momma. Daddy is in the bedroom with the door closed," Beverly told her.

"I'm going shopping at Sears and will call later. Tell Wendy and

Rodney not to worry about me; I'm fine."

When she called at five, Rodney said his father had just left.

"I'm on my way home. I have something to discuss with the three of you, so don't go anywhere."

So much has happened–so many depressing things have happened during the past few years. If I can pull my children and myself out of this living hell, things should start to get better. I hope and pray to God that things get better. There is not much room left for anything worse to occur.

Arriving home, Janice sat at the dining room table and called the children. Taking a long look at each of them before speaking, she said, "Today your father received a copy of the divorce petition my attorney and I filed with the court two weeks ago. I don't know how he's going to react when he sees me, but no matter what he does, please don't interfere. If what you see or hear is too upsetting for you, go to your rooms, close your doors, and turn on the radio or television. Promise me, each one of you–separately and individually–promise me you won't say anything."

Each of her children promised, one by one, as Janice turned her gaze upon them. The four of them heard a car I the drive. He's back! Her mind yelled when she heard the key in the lock.

Chris walked in and said, "Janice, we have to talk."

"We don't have anything to talk about. I have tried to talk to you for over a year, and you would not cooperate. It is too late for talk now."

Walking into the dining room he said, "We can talk here or we can go elsewhere and talk. Either way, we will talk. I'll tell you what, why don't you come and go with me on my rounds?" I still have a few clients to talk to. After I talk to them, we can stop and have a drink somewhere."

With a look on her face that told him to drop dead, Janice replied, "How nice of you to suggest I accompany you on your rounds. I have tried to get you to let me go with you on numerous occasions, but you wouldn't; now, because you have received notice of our doomed future, you want me to accompany you. No, I don't think so. I am remaining here."

Speaking close to her ear in a menacing voice, he whispered, "Do you want me to drag you out of here, or will you walk out without upsetting the children? I am going out to the car, and you had better follow me."

At this point, he turned on his heels and walked away. After he slammed the front door, Janice called the children into the dining room. "I am going with your father. I don't know where we will end up. Please call Minnie and tell her what has happened, and that I left with your father. I will call and let you know where I am if we are gone for a long time. I'll try and let you know every move we make." With this, she grabbed her purse and went outside.

"We are going in your car, I don't have any gas."

"You never have gas, to let you tell it." Park your car under the carport after I back out."

After parking his car under the carport, he said. "Let me drive. Since I know where my clients are, it will save time."

Leaving the last client's apartment, Chris said, "Honey, instead of going out for a drink, I think we should get a hotel room to discuss things in private. A bar or lounge would be crowded and we would most likely be disturbed by people we know."

"You can get a room if you have that kind of money, but I am telling you right now, I will not sleep in the same bed with you. If I did, that would void the divorce papers and I want this divorce so bad I can almost taste it."

Pulling into the parking lot of the Intercity Motel on Federal Highway, he said, "Wait here while I register."

Later as they entered the suite, the first thing she noticed was the large, overfilled waterbed. The center of the bed was so high it looked as if it was about to explode.

"You can sleep on that," she said pointing to the waterbed. I will sleep in the chair next to that monstrosity."

Continuing to look around, Janice noticed the mirrored ceiling and the television. Turning on the set she realized it was showing an X-rated movie. "I hope this thing shows more than X-rated movies. We are here to talk, not to make love."

"Janice, I still have a little work to do at the office. I'll be gone about an hour. Stay here until I return. I'll bring a pizza and drinks with me when I finish. You'll be alright until I return."

After he had been gone long enough, Janice left the room searching for a telephone booth. Calling her children she told them where Chris had rented a room for the night, and to call Minnie and inform her of their whereabouts.

Chris had been gone for three quarters of an hour when someone knocked on the door. "Who is it?" she asked in a frightened voice.

"The manager, ma'am, I've come to collect the money your husband owes for the room."

"Didn't my husband pay you?" she asked through a crack in the door.

"No, he promised to pay me in an hour, but he has not returned and it's time for me to go home."

"I'm sorry, I don't have any money and my husband has not returned. I will send him to the office as soon as he returns."

Hearing this he turned and left. A short time later, there came a loud banging on the door. "Who is it?" she asked.

"It's me, honey. Open the door," Chris yelled through the locked door. Opening the door, but keeping the safety chain in place, she made sure it was her husband. As she removed the chain and opened the door, Chris rushed past her, his arms loaded with a large pizza and four sodas.

Large beads of sweat were pouring down his face.

"I had to walk the last three blocks."

"Walk? What happened to my car? Where is my car?" she asked.

"It caught fire three blocks from here. Just as I crossed Andrews Avenue, a man yelled at me that the car was on fire. I pulled off the road and saw smoke coming from the back. I had heard a loud noise that sounded like a car backfiring as I crossed the highway, but I didn't realize it was your car. As I walked to the back the fire flamed up high. The man that stopped me came running with a fire extinguisher and put the fire out. The car is too damaged to be driven. It will have to be towed. It will probably be totaled by your insurance company. You do have insurance don't you?"

Janice stared at him, not believing the car had just caught on fire for no reason. He started the fire in my car because he is hoping to make me spend all the money I have saved. He can't find it but he knows me well enough to know I have money saved somewhere, and if I have to repair my car, he believes I won't have any money left for the divorce.

Wanting to yell and scream, she sat on the edge of the waterbed in a daze.

Finally, she asked, "How are we going to get home?"

Placing the pizza and drinks on the dresser, he said, "We'll spend the night and I'll call a taxi when we are ready to leave tomorrow. In the meantime, I'll go to the motel office and take care of some unfinished business."

Returning, he glanced at the television and said, "We don't want to watch "The Incredible Hunk' or any other regular show–let's watch an adult movie." He then switched the knob until he found a movie he wanted to watch.

Janice continued sitting in the chair next to the bed. As he began to undress he asked, "Aren't you going to undress?"

"No, I intend sleeping in this chair, in my clothes. I told you earlier I was going to sleep in this chair and I meant it. I want you to know I am very upset about my car and I don't fully understand what happened."

"We'll worry about the car tomorrow, now we have to discuss our future."

"Man, don't you understand anything? That paper you received today is the real thing. I am tired of trying to make this joke of a marriage work, so I'm giving up."

"Baby, don't do this to us. I am sorry for the things I've done. Please give me another chance to make things up to you and the children. I'll do better this time, I promise you. Look, why don't you take the bed and I'll sleep in the chair."

Leaning down, he pulled her up by her arms and sat her on the bed. Instead of releasing her, he started pulling at her clothing.

"Don't do that," she said pushing him away. "We came here to talk; or rather that is what I came here to do. If you don't want to talk, we can call a taxi now and not wait until tomorrow."

"Woman, you know you don't want a divorce. All you want is some of my good lovemaking and you will be all right. Let me undress you, like a good wife," he said, trying to tug her blouse over her head.

Pushing him away again and standing up, Janice said in a voice that was barely above a whisper, "If you insist on touching me, I will scream. I know what kind of place this is, but the management still won't want the people in the other rooms disturbed, so back off and leave me the hell alone."

Realizing she meant what she said, he pulled off his clothes and got into bed without another word. Th e next morning they arrived home, nothing had been discussed.

After much begging and pleading from Chris during the next month, Janice finally decided to give her marriage one more try. Chris had promised he would pay the bills on time and be faithful from this point on if Janice would only give their marriage one more chance.

On the first of April, she called Attorney Cline and asked him to put a hold on the divorce proceeding. She was going to give her husband one more chance to get their lives in order.

"Don't put the file in a dead-end cabinet, because I suspect it will be scheduled again rather soon. I am giving him one last chance to make this work, but I don't want to lose the money I paid your fi rm."

"All right Mrs. Blunt," the secretary said. "If you will look in the papers you received from us, you will see one that asks whether Mr. Blunt is in the armed forces or not. When you get ready to restart the proceedings, have that paper signed and notarized, and mail it to us. Th at will be our signal to restart the action and set up another court date."

Janice thanked the secretary and wondered for the hundredth time if she was making a big mistake.

Arriving home after a hard day at the office, Janice saw the mail in the green chair next to the front door. She checked through it and came upon the bank statement. Her heart began beating when she lifted the envelope. Directly beneath the envelope was a bulky letter from their mortgage company. Opening the envelope she saw the coupon book for their mortgage. Their payment had gone up to one hundred twenty-seven dollars a month. She quickly hid it in her purse, deciding to keep it in the drawer of her desk. She said nothing to Chris.

Th e next evening when Chris arrived home she told him. "I've decided from now on I'm going to make the mortgage payments and you can pay for our groceries."

"How much do you pay for groceries?" he asked. "Groceries cost around fifty dollars a week."

"I can't afford to pay fifty dollars a week for food. I'm keeping the house payment," he stated.

"I don't think so. We all have to eat. The mortgage has been late too many times and I'll not have my kids or me living on the street."

Noting the serious tone and look of his wife, he went into the bedroom without another word.

Chapter Twenty-Five

At first, everything seemed to be going fine. Mother's Day was coming and the FORT LAUDERDALE NEWS was full of advertisements for gifts. Reading the entertainment section, Janice saw that Dionne Warwicke and Peaches & Herb were appearing on the same bill at Sunrise Musical Theatre.

"Honey, do me a favor, Dionne and Peaches & Herb will be at the Sunrise Musical Theatre during Mother's Day weekend. Will you take me to see them? I would love to have a night out as my gift."

"Okay", he replied. "Dionne is one of my favorite entertainers."

Janice was so happy Chris agreed to take her to the show she went out and purchased a new outfit for the occasion.

Friday night, the beginning of the Mother's Day weekend, Janice asked Beverly to question her father on the date and time of the show at the theatre.

Walking into the kitchen where her father was standing, Beverly queried, "Daddy, what show are you taking Momma to this weekend?"

Glancing at his daughter, he replied, "Tend to your business and stop making trouble."

Holding her head down in embarrassment, Beverly turned and walked away.

Sunday afternoon, which was the big day, and the last day of the show at the theatre, Janice went into the kitchen where Chris was working on fishing tackle. "Honey, are we going to the theatre tonight? This is the last night for the show. Did you purchase the tickets?"

"What tickets are you talking about? I don't know anything about tickets for a show."

Janice felt a wave of weakness travel through the length of her entire body. How can he not remember the tickets for the show? He promised me that as my Mother's Day gift. Aloud, she said, "Chris, don't you remember you agreed to take me to the theatre as my gift for today?"

"I am not taking anyone in this damn house anywhere at any time, so get that through your head." With this, he pushed his way past her in the doorway and walked out.

Janice realized she was going through a conflict of emotions. She continued to feel as if she was the one in the wrong instead of Chris. Sometimes she'd think that if she had cooked his favorite meals more often, or said, "I love you" to him more, these troubled times would not have come about; she would still have a good marriage. In contrast, sometimes she would think about the electricity and the telephone being turned off, the first and second mortgage companies threatening foreclosure, and the loan company calling her at work threatening to take them to court if they did not make at least one payment on their overdue balance. Then she would become so incensed she could not stop imagining the look on Chris's face when the judge said, "Divorce granted. She wanted to pound some sense into him, but knew it was an impossible task.

One Sunday afternoon Chris was in the kitchen, Janice stood at the door that led from the dining room into the kitchen and asked, "Chris, why don't you hug me sometimes–put your arms around me and kiss me and tell me you love me? You told me you loved me to win my heart and it takes the same thing to keep me. I need to hear that. I need to feel your arms around me; I need to feel that you need and want me."

Chris looked at her and said, "I don't love or want anyone in this damn house," and walked out of the kitchen. The children were sitting in the den and heard this conversation, which made them cry. They felt hurt and ashamed for their mother.

Looking at her children with a forced smile and tears in her eyes, Janice said, "Don't pay any attention to him. He is under a lot of pressure right now, and does not realize what he said. Where is the Scrabble board?" she asked, trying to ease the tension in the room.

Later that night, Janice climbed into bed. Chris was on the far side of the queen-sized bed with his eyes closed, but Janice knew he was not asleep; his breathing was not that of a sleeping man. They had been married too long for her not to know the difference. Lying on her back wondering what to do, she turned toward him, put her arm across his chest and hugged him to her, kissing his shoulder.

"Leave me alone," he said. "I have a headache."

"Let's make love; it will make the headache go away," she replied, sliding her hand under the sheet.

"No, I don't feel well–my stomach is upset."

After an angry silence, Janice sat up and said, "Why the hell don't you go to her and get out of here?"

"Turn the damn light off and go to sleep!" he cried. As he moved away from her, he almost fell out of the bed. Getting up from the bed, he stormed out of the room. A few minutes later, she heard the television in the den.

What am I supposed to do? She wondered, and looked at the bookshelf in the corner. Getting up, she removed the Holy Bible from a shelf. I feel better, just touching this book. Lying down again, she wrapped her arms around the Bible, causing it to touch her breast. She fell asleep with the Good book clutched to her chest.

The next morning, Janice decided to go back to church. She dressed with a feeling of uneasiness. I have not been to a church in years, Chris never wanted to go and I changed my way of living to fit his lifestyle. I was reared in God's house. Now, I am ready to go back.

Half an hour later, looking at the church, Janice saw a large, cream-colored building with low-trimmed shrubbery and plenty of stained-glass windows. The parking lot, half full, was fenced in, a guard directing vehicles into parking slots. Pulling into the parking lot of First Baptist Church Piney Grove, Janice noticed a large crowd entering. There was a short sidewalk ending at the bottom of four steps that led up to double doors with dark-tinted glass.

She faltered as the crowd proceeded up the steps into the foyer. It had been years since she had been inside. Now, everything seemed new. An usher gave her a program and led her to a pew. Glancing around she saw plenty of familiar faces, but none she could immediately give a name.

Sitting on the pew, listening to the minister, it seemed he was speaking directly to her. He seemed to know of her inner troubles.

"Get your faith together," he said, "because you must live by your faith package when things get rough. Always be able to say, "This is what I live by; this is what I will die by." If you are right, God will fight your battles for you–if you are right. You must learn to let go and trust God. When you do let go and trust God, you don't have to worry anymore. And don't pick it up again; leave it with God, and continue on."

Hearing this, Janice knew she was on the right track. She had faith in herself, because she knew she had tried everything possible to make her failing marriage work.

Chapter Twenty-Six

Three months later, Janice realized Chris had used his last chance. Coming home from work, she noticed the children were not in their usual place–on the floor of the den, watching cartoons. Frowning, she walked around the unusually quiet house. Returning to the den she turned the television on, but nothing happened.

Walking into the bedroom where Chris as lying across the bed, she asked, "What's wrong with the television? I tried to turn it on and it didn't work. Do you have any idea what the problem is?"

Moving his arm from across his eyes, he said, "Florida Power & Light has turned the electricity off by mistake. I called them and they said a man would be out immediately. I raised hell with them because the bill has been paid. It's not my fault this time; they made the error."

Walking off, Janice thought, *'Like hell, FP&L made a mistake. The son- of-a-biscuit didn't pay the bill again'.* Continuing into the den she picked up the local section of the newspaper to read.

The lights were turned on around eight o'clock. Chris had left earlier, saying he had work at the office. After the FP&L employee had gone, Janice went into the master bedroom and looked around. I want that bank statement. I want proof that my thoughts are correct. She could not find where he had hidden the cancelled checks, but she noticed the plastic bag in the wastepaper basket was folded inside again. Unfolding the plastic, she again found two balled-up letters. One was from their bank, returning a check from FP&L due to insufficient funds, and one from Southern Bell, thanking him for the partial payment of the telephone bill, but stating that if the bill was not paid in full within two weeks, their service would be disconnected.

That same night, she moved into her son's bedroom. Rodney had a set of bunk beds, and she could no longer take the fighting and arguing she had been subjected to while remaining in the same bedroom with Chris.

One night, when Janice came home from a ceramics workshop, she found the house was dark. As she walked through the living room, the door to the master bedroom opened and Chris stepped out, asking her to come in and talk to him.

"There is nothing to talk about," she replied. "You've made it very clear that you do not want me."

Saying this, she turned to go into her son's room. Before she could walk away, Chris reached out, grabbed her by the arm, and dragged her into the master bedroom.

"If you touch me, I'll scream," Janice cried, "and you know the children will come from their rooms to find out why I am making so much noise."

Knowing that she would do just that, he released her. The next day, she had a talk with the children. Calling them to her, "Children, from now on, I want you to remain up until I get home. Whenever I go out at night, no matter how late I am, please don't go to bed."

"Momma, we didn't want to go to bed last night, but daddy made us," replied Rodney.

"This is the summer, and you don't have to go to school. If you are too sleepy to remain awake, lie on the sofa in the living room. Remember, whatever you do, don't go to bed until I'm home. If your father insists you go to bed, the three of you remain together in the living room. He won't bother you if the three of you refuse to go to bed. Also, I will no longer cook, clean, or do laundry. The four of us will eat out, you will clean up after yourselves, and you will wash your own clothes. I hate to make you stay up when you're sleepy, but I will not be going out too often."

The children knew they had no choice about doing what their mother had asked. They also knew that their father would not insist they go to bed if the three of them said they wanted to remain up until their mother returned.

A few nights later, Janice and the children were in bed when Chris came home. Half an hour after he arrived home, Janice heard the knob rattle on the closed bedroom door. The next thing she knew, the door slowly opened. Turning to glance at the door, she saw Chris walk into the room.

"What do you want?" she asked, knowing as she looked at him that he had been drinking.

"Tell me something," he said. "What is rehabilitation?"

"Rehabilitation is another word for alimony. Now if that is all you want, get out of here, I'm sleepy."

"Sleepy," he said standing over her as she looked up from the lower bunk, "I'll put you to sleep for good." He raised his hand to strike her.

As Chris raised his hand, Rodney sat up and said, "Who is making all this noise in here?" I can't sleep." Seeing his father in the room, he asked, "Daddy, what's wrong?"

Realizing his son was awake; Chris lowered his fist and said to Janice. "You can have this damn house, but I won't pay you one red cent in alimony. Take my half of this house; I never wanted it to begin with. You are the one who wanted it." With these words, he turned and reeled out of the room. A few minutes later, they heard the door to his bedroom slam shut.

The next day, Janice called Attorney Cline and told him what her husband had done and what he had said. Attorney Cline questioned her about the lock on the door, then suggested that since the lock on the bedroom door was so easy to pick, she purchased a lock for inside the door and locked herself in at night.

That weekend, Janice and the children went to the flea market where she purchased both a lock and a brace for the lock.

Going to bed that Friday night, she felt safe for the first time in weeks. Around three o'clock in the morning, she heard Chris come home. He did not stop at his bedroom, but continued to the door of Rodney's bedroom. After trying to open the door with a toothpick, he realized the knob turned, but the door had remained tightly shut. She heard him swear and walk away.

The next morning while she and the children were in the den, they saw Chris come out of his bedroom and walk to the other side of the house. Looking at each other, they knew he was going to check why he could not open the door. A few minutes later, he walked back into his bedroom and closed the door.

Chapter Twenty-Seven

Janice had asked her supervisor, Bessie Collins, to be her residency witness at the divorce hearing. On September 26, 1980 as they walked down the short hallway toward the judge's chambers, Janice said, "Bessie, I am so scared my insides are shaking like Jell-O."

Placing an arm around Janice's shoulders, Bessie replied, "I know you are scared. What is about to take place may be very emotional and unpleasant for you. Take a deep breath and count to ten as you slowly expel it."

When they entered and looked around the packed waiting room, two older men stood, allowing them to sit. Thinking the gentlemen with smiles, they quickly sat.

"Chris is not here yet," she whispered to Bessie. "Maybe he won't show up."

"Don't worry, he will be here. I really don't think he believes you are going through with the divorce," Bessie replied.

"He doesn't think I am going through with it. His brother told me before I left this morning that Chris had told his mother and aunt that I was not serious. He thinks I am going to let the proceedings go almost to the end, then tell the judge that I feel he has learned his lesson and I no longer want the divorce. None of his family believes I am serious. They all believe that a man can do whatever he wants to do and apologize only when he is caught. The woman is supposed to continually forgive and forget, because men will be men."

At this point, Chris walked into the room and asked to speak to Janice outside. He was dressed in a three piece dark green polyester suit. Sitting straighter and squaring her shoulders, but unable to keep her voice from trembling, she said, "We have nothing to discuss."

"Janice, please step outside for a minute. There is something I must say to you," he said, reaching down and pulling her up by the elbow.

Not wanting to cause a scene, she reluctantly walked to the door. As they reached the hallway, he immediately jerked her around to face him. Wrapping her in his arms he said, "Baby, why do you have to do this to the family? You are destroying everything we have worked for. Please reconsider, don't break this family apart."

Jerking out of his arms, she cried. "Don't do that! Don't you dare shift the blame for this failed marriage to me! I have tried everything I know to make a go of this farce, while all you ever did was spend our money on your women and their children. Our children did without while you spent your salary on her and her children. Take your filthy hands off me before I hit you with my fist."

Dropping his hands to his side, Chris realized there was no talking to her.

He watched as she stormed back into the waiting room.

A short while later, Janice and Chris were sitting in the inner sanctum of the judge's chamber.

The judge began, "Mrs. Blunt, you are asking for custody of a child and support for this child. Is that correct?"

"It is, Your Honor," replied Attorney Cline, responding for Janice.

Turning to Chris, the judge said, "Mr. Blunt, can you afford to pay child support of twenty-five dollars per week for your child?"

"Yes, sir, I can pay whatever she wants me to pay," he answered.

"The court finds that the petitioner is the fit and proper person to have the custody of the child of the parties, and therefore custody of the minor child of the parties, Rodney Blunt, be and hereby is awarded to the petitioner, with reasonable rights of visitation to the husband, that the husband pay unto the wife the sum of twenty-five dollars per week as an for child support until such time child of the parties, Rodney Blunt, reaches the age of eighteen or to otherwise legally emancipated.

"Now, on the next item on the list, Mr. Blunt, Mrs. Blunt is asking for your half of the house in lieu of alimony. What do you have to say about that?"

"She can have it," Chris replied.

Upon hearing this, the judge said, "Mr. Blunt, how long have you lived in this house?"

"Twelve years, Your Honor," he answered.

"How much did the house cost?" the judge asked, also at what percent of interest, and how much was the down-payment?"

After hearing the answers to these questions, the judge reached into a drawer. Placing a calculator on the table top, he began to punch the keys. Presently, he said, "Mr. Blunt, do you realize that giving up your share of the house is like giving her almost seventeen thousand-dollars in cash do you realize what you are doing?"

Peering into Janice's face, Chris asked, "Do you want it?"

Crying, shaking like a leaf in a strong wind, she replied in a small voice, "Yes." She was too scared to say more than that one word, but in her mind she was begging, Please God, let him give me the house. He never wanted it anyway.

Chris turned back to the judge, saying, "Give it to her."

"Mr. Blunt, I am asking you one more time; do you know what you are doing?"

Hearing this, Janice thought, He should not be doing this; he is trying to stop Chris from giving me the house. Just because he is too dumb to hire an attorney to represent him is no reason for the judge to continue trying to get him to think of the consequences of his actions. I know exactly what he is doing; he is gambling on the fact that I don't believe in divorce. He doesn't realize I am going to call his bluff.

"I know what I'm doing judge, give her the house," Chris said. Sitting up straight in his plush chair, the judge said. "The property is hereby awarded to the wife. This award is made as and for a lump-sum alimony."

Hearing this, Janice signed and relaxed.

"Mr. Blunt, the next item is attorney fees. Mrs. Blunt is asking you to pay her attorney. Can you pay his fee?"

"No, sir, I can't," Chris said in a strong voice.

"Mrs. Blunt, he cannot pay your attorney fees. What do you have to say?"

Taking a deep breath and letting it out slowly, she replied, "Judge, I don't have that kind of money."

"Just a moment judge," Attorney Cline said, as he jotted figures on the inside cover of the manila folder he was holding. "I'll waive my fees where Mr. Blunt is concerned."

The judge immediately said, "Claim for attorney fees, rehabilitative alimony, and court costs is hereby denied." At this point, the bailiff walked to the judge and whispered into his ear.

"I'm calling five minutes recess," said the judge. After the recess, the judge asked, "Mr. Blunt do you have anything to say on your behalf?"

"Yes, I do judge. I love my family," Chris said as he stood, walking around the room, beating his fist against the books on the shelves lining the walls around the judge's chambers. He walked and struck the books, shaking his head as if he could not believe what was happening to him.

"I don't want this divorce." At this point, he leaned across the table, looked directly at Janice, saying, "Baby, now that I have given you everything I possess in this world, why don't we stop this foolishness and go home?"

"Mrs. Blunt, you have been married for almost nineteen years. I have a marriage counseling program that meets once a week. Would you and Mr. Blunt consider attending sessions for the thirty day trial period and if you still want a divorce, I will grant it without delay."

"Judge, I don't want to sound disrespectful, but weren't you listening to him earlier? He told you that during the months of April to August, I had stopped the divorce action. But he was on probation, and because of this probation, he felt as if he were being treated like a child and deliberately allowed his salary to drop to almost nothing. Do you seriously believe another try will help improve the situation? I don't think another trial will help, and no, sir, I would not like to participate in your program."

As she talked, Janice almost squeezed Bessie's hand in two.

"Yes, baby," Chris anxiously cried out, I am willing to give it another try if you are."

Mr. Blunt, the judge said, "I don't seem to be able to convince her. Why don't you give it a try?"

Before Chris could again speak, Janice said, "There is not enough molasses in the world to talk me into going back to a situation like the one I have tried so hard to get out of."

Realizing it was useless to try to save this marriage, the judge said, "Mr. Blunt, you have thirty days in which to execute a quit-claim deed transferring all rights, title, and interest in the aforesaid real property. You must also vacate the premises of said real property within ten days of the date of this hearing." Turning to Janice, he continued, "Mrs. Blunt, if he has not vacated the premises after ten days, you have the legal right to call the sheriff and have him removed. The divorce is granted and this hearing is adjourned."

Walking down the short corridor of the courthouse, Bessie asked Janice, "Where do you go from here?"

Looking at her friend and co-worker, tears streaming down her lovely pecan tan face, she replied, "Up, Bessie, up."

Two weeks after the divorce, Janice received a letter from Attorney Cline informing her that he had waived his fee as far as Mr. Blunt was concerned, but she was not exempt. He wanted her to pay him $425, the remaining cost of the divorce. She became very angry as she read the letter.

"I told that man I could not afford to pay for the divorce. If he was dumb enough to waive his fee, that is no concern of mine," she furiously muttered as she threw the letter on the table and dialed his office.

"May I speak to Attorney Cline?" she asked the receptionist. Getting him on the telephone, she said without greeting, "I refuse to give any thought to paying your firm one red cent. I told you in the beginning I could not afford to pay for my divorce. You took it upon yourself to waive your fee. If your firm wants your fee paid, sue me."

"We will Mrs. Blunt," he replied, recognizing her voice. "If you refuse to pay us we will take you to court."

"You can't get blood from a turnip," she said and slammed down the receiver.

Two months later, Janice found herself standing before a judge. The judge leaned across his desk and asked, "Mrs. Blunt, do you know why you are here?"

"I am being sued for attorney fees. Judge, I told him in the beginning I couldn't afford to pay his fees, and I requested my husband pay for the divorce. Attorney Cline waived his fee during the divorce hearing."

Looking at Janice, the judge replied, "From what I am reading in these papers, Attorney Cline waived his fee as to your husband paying them. I see nowhere that Attorney Cline waived his fees where you are concerned. Your husband does not have to pay; you do."

Reaching toward the judge, Janice said, "Look at this, Judge. I am stuck with paying a second mortgage on the house. My ex-husband agreed to pay off one of the two major bills we have and I agreed to pay off the second mortgage, which is the larger of the two bills. I cannot afford to pay this man too."

Taking the paper from her hand, the judge glanced at the paper and asked Attorney Cline, "Have you seen this?"

"No, your honor, I know nothing about that paper," Attorney Cline said, reaching to take the paper from the judge's hand.

"I suggest the two of you go out into the hallway or to the back of this courtroom and work out your problem; you do seem to have a problem. If I have to make a decision, I will have to issue a final judgment in favor of the law firm, Mrs. Blunt. You will have to pay."

Attorney Cline and Janice walked out into the hallway to discuss their problem.

"Attorney Cline," Janice said as soon as the courtroom door closed behind them, "I am a professional typist. I cannot afford to pay you in cash, but I could come to your firm's office and type for the firm on weekends. That is the only way I can think of to pay you," she said hoping he realized that typing services were the only services she was offering.

"I will have to talk to my boss before I can answer that, but if you don't pay our fee, we can put a lien on your house. You got that in the divorce settlement," he stated. "My boss was very upset with me for waiving my fee, and I have to reach some kind of a settlement to satisfy him."

"I know what you can do," Janice said with excitement in her voice. "Since I have no intentions of ever selling the property and you can't get your money unless I sell it, we can do this: Sue my ex-husband for contempt of court. He is supposed to pay me twenty-five dollars per week in child support, but he doesn't. He paid the first two weeks after the divorce and refuses to pay anymore. Whatever the court makes him pay, I will turn it over to you as your fee. How does that sound?"

"I will take your suggestion to my boss and then get back in touch with you," he replied as he walked toward the bank of elevators.

Two days later Attorney Cline called Janice. Their law firm would be suing Mr. Christopher Blunt, on her behalf, for contempt of court. Janice was elated. A little pressure had been lifted; she had been worried where the money would come from if she had to pay for the divorce. Bringing herself up short, she thought, don't get too happy yet. The judge may not do a darn thing about Chris not paying child support.

Two months later, Janice walked out of the Broward County Courthouse smiling from ear to ear. The judge had ordered Chris to pay half the back child support he owed Janice. At first she was angry because he did not have to pay the full amount, but when Attorney Cline told her he was sure his firm would be satisfied with that amount, she was happy.

Walking with a swing to her hips, she said for the world to hear, "Now to get on with my life."